AT THE STROKE OF MIDNIGHT

At the Stroke of Midnight

TRADITIONAL FAIRY TALES RETOLD BY

Helen Cresswell

ILLUSTRATED BY CAROLYN DINAN

COLLINS *St James's Place, London*

For Caroline with love

ISBN 0 00 195041 X
Text Helen Cresswell 1971
©Illustrations William Collins Sons & Co. Ltd.
© First published 1971
Printed in Great Britain
Collins Clear-Type Press
London and Glasgow

Author's Note

When I lost the attention of my four year-old daughter for the fifth time during a reading of Aladdin I became suspicious. Four year-olds are supposed to *like* Aladdin. The next night I told her the story of Aladdin in my own words. She listened. She was ready for the message but not, it seemed, for the medium. The schism between style and content was too wide. I did not believe that my own four or five or six year-old self had read these versions, or had even been told them aloud. I must have read Someone-or-Other's version. And it was at this point that I thought, 'All right, if it's got to be somebody's version, it might as well be mine.'

Then I began to look more closely at some of these old fairy stories in the original, and to wonder whether they could be simplified without sacrilege, whether a few (dare it be whispered?) might even be improved? Though I approached the task with something like awe. (In fact, *with* awe.) These stories were part of the landscape of my own childhood, fixed and unalterably there, seeming beyond change as anything else that has happened in the past.

What I have done is to rewrite these stories for telling aloud to young children. Fairy tales are best told aloud to young children. Fairy tales are best told aloud first – best for a child to share with an adult the wonder, terror, sadness and delight that are roused on the first encounters with stories whose age is proof of their power. Because after all, there will be other times, other tellings. No child reads fairy tales only once. They are like the grit in the oyster, and over the years each child will make his own private pearl. Making pearls is an intensely private affair.

The two principal things I aimed for in retelling these tales were simplicity and closeness to the spirit of the original (two aims not always easy to reconcile as any reader of original versions will know). I have aimed too at a pictorial telling – the suggestion of a landscape of fairy tale where the magical and the real meet – a black bird walking stiffly on the snow, a golden glow in a stone cell, the smell of nettles in the twilight.

I hope that I have made grit, and that from it many children will make pearls.

H.C.

Contents

Little Red Riding Hood

ONCE upon a time there was a little girl whose father was a woodcutter in a great forest. Her mother had made her a cloak and hood of bright red wool, and she wore it so often that she was known as Little Red Riding Hood.

One day her mother called her and said,

'Your grandmother is not well today. I have made some little cakes and put them in this basket, and there's a pat of butter and some new laid eggs. I want you to take them to her and see how she is. But mind you go straight there and back, and don't go off the path.'

Red Riding Hood was very fond of her grandmother and gladly set off along the path that led to her cottage. It was a fine, sunny day and wild flowers were blooming all about, so after a while Little Red Riding Hood thought,

'It's early in the day, and there's plenty of time. And I would only have to step a *little* way off the path to pick some of these flowers. I could take them to Grandmother to make her feel better.'

So she wandered off the path and began picking flowers, and was soon deep in the wood. In the distance she could hear the blows of the woodcutters' axes and sometimes their voices, singing while they worked. But the Wolf of the Wood was lurking nearby, spying from behind a tree.

'This looks a juicy morsel,' thought he. 'But I dare not eat

her here, the woodcutters are too near. I will speak to her, and find out where she is going.'

So he came out from behind the tree and said as softly as he could, 'Good day, little girl. Are you walking the same way as me? Perhaps I could carry your basket for you, so that you can pick flowers more easily?'

'Thank you kindly, sir,' replied Little Red Riding Hood. 'But I am going to my Grandmother's cottage, just along the path to the other side of the wood. And as I'm nearly there, I won't put you to any trouble.'

'Good day, then,' said the wolf politely. 'I hope that we shall meet again soon.'

He hoped so very much indeed, and Little Red Riding Hood had not noticed the wicked glint in his eye when she told him where she was going.

She picked another handful of buttercups and daisies, then set off down the path again towards her Grandmother's cottage.

When she knocked at the door, a hoarse voice called out,

'Lift the latch, and the door will open. Come right in, my dear!'

Little Red Riding Hood lifted the latch and went in. She saw her Grandmother lying in bed wearing a big frilled night-cap and with the blankets pulled up to her chin.

'I'm sorry to find you in bed, Grandmother,' said she. 'I've brought you some cakes that Mother has baked, and a pat of butter and some new laid eggs. And here are some flowers I picked myself to cheer you up and make your room look gay.'

'The Wolf (for the Wolf it was, under the frilled lace nightcap) told her to put the food in the pantry and to arrange the flowers in a vase.

'Now you must come and lie beside me and rest,' he said, when Red Riding Hood had finished.

She went up close to the bed, and thought how strangely her Grandmother had changed now that she was sick.

'O Grandmother, what great ears you have!' she said.

'All the better to hear you with, my dear,' said the Wolf.

'O Grandmother, what great eyes you have,' said Little Red Riding Hood.

'All the better to see you with, my dear,' replied the Wolf.

'O Grandmother, what great arms you have,' cried Red Riding Hood.

'All the better to hug you with, my dear,' said the Wolf, and he stretched them out towards her, but Red Riding Hood stepped quickly back and gasped,

'O Grandmother, what great *teeth* you have!'

'The better to eat you with!' cried the Wolf then, and he sprang up from the bed to devour her. But just then a wasp flew through the open window and stung him on the nose. The Wolf let out a great yowl, and as he howled the door opened and an arrow flew straight in and pierced the wicked Wolf through and through.

Little Red Riding Hood turned and saw, standing in the doorway with his bow in hand, the Green Archer, who was keeper of the forest for the King.

'I saw you talking with the wicked Wolf, little maid,' he said, 'and came to save you. Your Grandmother is safe and sound at my house. It was Puck the fairy who changed himself into the wasp and made the Wolf howl as a signal for me to shoot my arrow. For I don't like little girls to be eaten up, even when they do disobey their mothers and wander away from the path and speak with wolves.'

Little Red Riding Hood's face turned so red that it almost matched her cloak.

'I shall never do it again,' she promised. And she never did.

13

The Three Billygoats Gruff

THERE were once three Billy-Goats who lived on a green mountain side. They all had rough grey coats and wispy beards. They all had nimble, skipping feet and they were all excessively fond of daisies – to eat. They were called Littlest Billy-Goat Gruff, Middle Billy-Goat Gruff and Biggest Billy-Goat Gruff.

At the bottom of the valley where they lived ran a river, and over the river was a bridge. And under the bridge lived a very unpleasant Troll, with big flashing eyes, far too many teeth, and a long, twitching, sharp-as-a-needle nose. And the Troll was excessively fond of Billy-goats – to eat.

The Three Billy-Goats Gruff were happy enough on their own side of the river, but sometimes, when they lay in an evening gazing over to the other side, it seemed to them as if the grass there was just a *teeny* shade greener than their own grass, and a *teeny* shade longer. It was hard to tell from such a long way off, but the daisies looked a shade larger, too.

So one day, Littlest Billy-Goat Gruff set off to try the grass on the other side of the valley. Down he skipped till he came to the bridge, then over the bridge itself, trip trap, trip trip trap.

'Ho!' came a deep voice from under the bridge. 'Ho! I'm a troll, and I live in a hole under the bridge! Who goes there?'

'It's me! It's me, sir! Littlest Billy-Goat Gruff! I'm off to try the long green grass on the other side, and grow big and fat!'

'Ho!' cried the Troll again. 'Ho no you're not! *I'm* going to eat *you* and grow big and fat!'

'Don't do that! Don't do that!' cried Littlest Billy-Goat Gruff. 'There's hardly a mouthful of me, really there's not!

I'm so little and skinny I'd be gone in a swallow! Wait for my
brother, he's much bigger than I am. He's got four of the fattest
legs you've ever seen, and you could make a *real* meal out of
him!'

'Ho! He has, has he?' roared the Troll. 'Be off, then, I'll
wait for him! Yum! Youm! Yum!'

The Littlest Billy-Goat Gruff skipped smartly off before the
troll could change his mind, and soon he was gobbling daisies
big as saucers.

Not long after, Middle Billy-Goat Gruff came up to the
bridge and began to go across, trip trap, trip trip trap.

'Ho!' roared the Troll. 'Who goes there?'

'It's me! It's me, sir, Middle Billy-Goat Gruff! I'm off to the other side to eat the long green grass and grow big and fat!'

'Ho! Ho no you're not! *I'm* going to eat *you* and grow big and fat!'

'I shouldn't do that!' cried Middle Billy-Goat Gruff. 'I shouldn't do that, sir! You'd be disappointed in me. I'm no size at all for a fellow like you. My brother who's coming along soon, he's twice the size of me. Enormous! You could make a meal out of his tail alone!'

'Ho? Really? Then I'll wait,' growled the Troll. 'But I'm getting hungrier, and *hungrier* and HUNGRIER, here under this bridge! Be off!'

Middle Billy-Goat Gruff galloped sharply off before the Troll could change his mind.

Presently, along came Biggest Billy-Goat Gruff, trip trap, trip trip trap over the bridge.

'Ho!' roared the Troll, who by now was ravenous and ready to eat *ten* goats. '*Ho*! Who goes there?'

'It's me, Biggest Billy-Goat Gruff. I'm off to eat the juicy grass over on the other side, and grow big and fat.'

'Ho no you're not! roared the Troll, jumping out from under the bridge. '*I'm* going to eat *you* and grow big and fat!'

'*Oh* no, you're not!' retorted Biggest Billy-Goat Gruff, and he ran at the Troll and caught him on his great curly horns and tossed him right up into the air like a pancake. The troll let out a loud bellow and came down splash into the river.

'Serve him right,' said Biggest Billy-Goat Gruff. 'Great big bullying greedy old Troll!'

And he trotted on over the bridge to join his brothers and the three of them ate and ate and ate until daisies came out of their ears.

The Three Little Pigs

ONCE upon a time a Mother Sow had three little pigs. There was never enough food to go round the four of them, so one day she sent them out into the world to make their own way.

The first little pig met a man with a cartload of straw.

'Man, man, give me some straw. I want to build myself a house.'

So the man gave him some straw, and the little pig built himself a house. Then he sat inside it, very warm and snug and pleased with himself.

Presently, along came a wolf.

'*Little pig, little pig, let me come in!*'

'*No, by the hair on my chinny chin chin!*'

The little pig had heard tales about the wolf from his mother, and had not liked the sound of him at all.

'*Then I'll huff, and I'll puff, and I'll blow your house down!*' said the wolf.

So he huffed, and he puffed, and he blew the house down and gobbled the little pig right up.

The second little pig was trotting along when he met a man with a cartload of twigs.

'Man, man, give me some twigs. I want to build myself a house.'

So the man gave him some twigs, and the little pig built himself a house and sat inside it feeling very comfortable and safe.

Presently, along came the wolf.

'*Little pig, little pig, let me come in!*'

'*No, by the hair on my chinny chin chin!*'

This little pig was just as particular about his visitors as his brother had been.

'*Then I'll huff, and I'll puff, and I'll blow your house down!*' said the wolf.

And he huffed and he puffed, and he puffed and he huffed and at last he blew the house right down and gobbled up the little pig.

The third little pig was rooting about for acorns when he met a man with a cartload of bricks.

'Man, man, give me some bricks. I want to build myself a house.'

So the man gave him some bricks, and the little pig built himself a fine house with a real chimney and a front door with a knocker. Then he went and sat inside, feeling very proud and pleased.

Presently, along came the wolf.

'*Little pig, little pig, let me come in!*'

'*No, by the hair on my chinny chin chin!*'

This little pig didn't mean to be taken in by a wolf, either.

'*Then I'll huff, and I'll puff, and I'll blow your house down!*' said the wolf.

'Huff away!' replied the little pig. 'Puff away! See if I care!'

Well, the wolf huffed and he puffed, and he puffed and he huffed. Then he had a little rest, then he began again. He huffed and he puffed and he puffed and he huffed, and not a scrap of difference did it make. In the end, the wolf saw that he could puff all the breath out of his body and still not get in, so he thought up another plan to catch the pig.

'Listen, little pig,' said he. 'I know where there's a whole field full of turnips.'

'Where?' said the pig.

'In Farmer Brown's ten acre,' said the wolf. 'You get up at six o'clock tomorrow and wait for me here. Then I'll call for you, and we'll go and get some turnips for dinner.'

'That will be very nice,' said the little pig. 'I'll see you at six o'clock tomorrow, then,'

But next morning he got up at *five* o'clock and went to Farmer Brown's Ten Acre and filled a big sack full of turnips, enough to last him a week. Then he went back home to his little brick house. At six o'clock along came the wolf and banged on the knocker.

'Are you ready, little pig?' he called.

'Ready?' replied the pig. 'I've been to Farmer Brown's field and back already, and there's enough turnips in my larder to last me a week!'

The wolf ground his teeth at this and itched to get them into the juicy little pig. But he still had another trick up his sleeve.

'Little pig! I know where there's an apple tree full of red apples!'

'Oh? Where?' said the pig.

'Down at Merry-garden,' replied the wolf. 'You meet me here at five o'clock tomorrow morning, and I'll take you there.'

Next morning the little pig was up by *four* o'clock and went down to Merry-garden with a big basket to collect apples. But they were so red and ripe that he kept stopping to eat one and forgot all about the time. He was still up in the tree when along came the wolf.

'Good day, little pig,' said the wolf, showing his teeth. He thought he had caught the little pig properly this time. 'Are they nice apples?'

'Very!' replied the little pig. 'Here, I'll throw one down for you!'

He threw one, but he threw it so far that while the wolf was chasing after it the little pig was able to scramble down the tree and run off home as fast as his trotters would carry him.

The wolf, as you may be sure, was furious. His fur fairly bristled with rage and he was more determined than ever to get his teeth into that tricky little pig.

Next day he went back to the house and banged the knocker.

'Little pig, there's a fair this afternoon at Shanklin. Do you want to go?'

'O yes,' said the little pig, without opening the door. 'I like fairs. What time shall we go?'

'At three,' replied the wolf. 'Be ready, and I'll call for you.'

But once again the little pig set off early. He went to the fair and had a good time and bought a butter churn which he rolled before him along the road towards home.

But he was only half way home when he saw the wolf coming towards him up the hill. The little pig got inside the churn and gave it a push and began to bowl helter skelter down the road, rattling and banging like a kettle drum, straight at the wolf. The wolf was so terrified that he put his tail down and ran home without stopping once, and didn't get to the fair at all.

When he was feeling a little better, the wolf set off again for the pig's house, and told him how he had been going to

23

the fair when a great huge round thing had come bowling
down the hill at him and nearly squashed him flat.

'Oh, that would be me, inside my butter churn!' said the
little pig. 'I'd already been to the fair, and was on my way
home. Frightened you out of your wits, did I? Ha! Ha! I must
laugh. Ha! ha!'

The wolf gnashed his teeth terribly then, and determined
that come what may he *would* eat that little pig, and eat him
that very day.

'The only way in is down the chimney,' he thought. 'So
that is the way I'll go.'

But the little pig saw what he was up to, and straightway
lit a blazing fire and hung a pot of water over it. Then he sat
and waited, and just as the wolf came hurtling down the
chimney, he took the lid off the pot and splash! – in went the
wolf!

The little pig boiled him up for supper with some of Farmer
Brown's turnips, with an apple to follow. And needless to say,
he lived happily ever afterwards.

The Gingerbread Boy

ONCE upon a time there was a little old woman who was making gingerbread. This old woman had never had any children of her own and had always longed for a little boy. So she said to her husband,

'I will make a little boy out of gingerbread. I'll knead the dough, and roll it, and cut out just the shape I want. Then I'll give him currants for his eyes and a slice of orange peel for a mouth, and I'll pop him in the oven and when he's nicely baked I'll take him out and I'll have a little boy of my own at last!'

The husband shook his head at his wife's words, and went off to work in the field outside. The old woman did exactly what she had said she would do. She kneaded and rolled and

shaped, and when at last the gingerbread boy was cooked she opened the oven door to take him out.

Before she could even blink out popped the little gingerbread boy of his own accord. He jumped out of the oven, ran out through the kitchen door and when he was in the street looked back over his shoulder and shouted,

'*Run, run as fast as you can,*
You can't catch me, I'm the gingerbread man!'

'Husband, husband, come quick!' cried the little old woman. And her husband came running from the field and they both ran after the gingerbread boy but they couldn't catch him.

As for the little gingerbread boy, he went running on and

on till he met a cow eating daisies in a meadow. When the
cow saw the little gingerbread boy, she said,

'Moo! Moo! *You* look good to eat! Stop, stop, little gingerbread boy, and let me eat you up!'

But the gingerbread boy only laughed and ran faster than
ever, and as he ran he shouted over his shoulder,

'I have run away from a little old man and a little old
woman, and I can run away from you, I can!

'*Run, run, as fast as you can,*
You can't catch me, I'm the gingerbread man!'

The cow began to lumber after him, but she had eaten too
many buttercups, and she couldn't catch him, either. So on and

on he ran till he came to a horse drinking from a trough by the wayside. When the horse saw the little gingerbread boy he said,

'Neigh! Neigh! *You* look good to eat! Stop, stop, little gingerbread boy, and let me eat you up!'

But the gingerbread boy only laughed and ran faster than ever, and as he ran he shouted over his shoulder,

'I have run away from a little old man and a little old woman and a big fat cow, and I can run away from you, I can!

'*Run, run as fast as you can,*
You can't catch me, I'm the gingerbread man!'

And the horse began to gallop after him, but he couldn't catch him, either. The little gingerbread boy ran on and on

till he came to some haymakers working in a field. They all began to shout to him,

'Hey, hey! *You* look good to eat! Stop, stop, little gingerbread boy, and let us eat you up!'

But the little gingerbread boy only laughed and ran faster than ever, and as he ran he shouted over his shoulder,

'I have run away from a little old man and a little old woman, and a big fat cow and a horse, and I can run away from you, I can!

'*Run, run, as fast as you can,*
You can't catch me, I'm the gingerbread man!'

And the haymakers threw down their pitchforks and began to run after him, but they couldn't catch him, either.

The little gingerbread boy ran on and on till he came to a river, and then he *had* to stop, because he didn't know how to swim. As he sat there wondering what he should do, along came a fox. The fox thought the little gingerbread boy looked good enough to eat, too, but he was clever enough not to say so. Instead, he grinned and showed his big yellow teeth, and said,

'Do you want to go across the river?'

'Yes, I do,' said the little gingerbread boy.

'Jump on my back, then,' invited the fox. 'I can swim, and I'll take you across.'

So the little gingerbread boy climbed on the fox's back and the fox began to swim across the river. When he was half way over, the fox called out,

'You might get wet on my back, little gingerbread boy. Jump up on to my neck.'

So the little gingerbread boy climbed on the fox's neck and the fox swam a bit further. Then he called out again,

'It can't be very comfortable clinging to my neck, little gingerbread boy. Jump on my head.'

So the little gingerbread boy jumped on the fox's head and clung on tightly and the fox swam a bit further. Then he called out again,

'We're nearly there, now! Climb on to the tip of my nose for the rest of the way, you'll be safer there!'

So the little gingerbread boy climbed on to the tip of the fox's nose. And then the fox threw back his head and went 'Snap' with his snapping jaws, and the little gingerbread boy was half gone. Then the fox did it again – 'snap' – and the little gingerbread boy was three quarters gone. Then the fox did it once more – 'Snap!' (oh, he was enjoying himself!) – and after that the little gingerbread boy was all gone. And that was the end of the gingerbread biscuit boy who had out-witted a little old man and a little old woman and a cow and a horse and a field full of haymakers, but hadn't been quite clever enough to outwit a fox!

Goldilocks and the Three Bears

ONCE upon a time a family of bears lived in a house in a wood. There was a Great Rough Bear (who was the father), a Middle-sized Bear (who was the mother) and a Wee Small Bear (who was the baby, of course). They were very good bears, and the Green Huntsman who kept the forest for the King, often gave them honey from the wild bees' nest when there was some left over.

One day Mother Bear made some porridge, which was their favourite dish. It was too hot to eat, and because they could not bear to sit looking at it as it steamed deliciously in their bowls, they set off for a short walk in the wood.

'When we come back, it will be just right to eat,' said Mother Bear.

No sooner had they gone when a little girl called Goldilocks

came wandering by, picking flowers. She saw the little house, and went to the door and knocked. There was no reply, of course, and as the door was standing a little way open, she gave it a push and went inside. The first thing she saw was the table set with the steaming bowls of porridge.

'I'll sit down and try some,' she thought. 'Nobody seems to want it, and it seems a pity to waste it.'

She sat on the biggest chair, but it was too big. She tried Mother Bear's chair, but that was still too big. Then she sat on the wee small chair and crash, the legs broke and the chair and Goldilocks went tumbling to the floor together.

'O dear!' said Goldilocks. But she was still determined to try the porridge, so she went all round the table, tasting from each bowl.

First she tried the bowl belonging to the Great Rough Bear – because that one was the biggest. It was too hot. So was the porridge in Mother Bear's bowl, but when she came to the last one, belonging to the Wee Small Bear, it was just right, and she ate it all up. She had not *meant* to eat it all, but it was so delicious that she just went on tasting and tasting till it had all gone.

'I'm tired now after my long walk,' said Goldilocks. 'I must find somewhere to rest.'

She went upstairs and lay on the bed belonging to the Great Rough Bear, but it was too big, and she couldn't settle. Then she tried Mother Bear's bed, but that wasn't right either. But when she lay on the Wee Small Bear's bed it felt exactly right, and she was so comfortable that soon she was fast asleep.

Not long after, the three bears came home from their walk.

'Someone's been sitting on my chair,' growled the Great Rough Bear in his great rough voice.

'Someone's been sitting in my chair, too,' said Mother Bear in her soft mother voice.

'Someone's been sitting in my chair and broken it all to pieces!' cried the Wee Small Bear in his small shrill voice.

'Someone's been tasting my porridge,' growled the Great Rough Bear in his great rough voice.

'Someone's been tasting my porridge, too,' said the Mother Bear in her soft mother voice.

'Someone has been tasting my porridge and has tasted it all up!' cried the Wee Small Bear in his shrill small voice.

Then the bears went upstairs.

'Someone has been lying in my bed,' growled the Great Rough Bear in his great rough voice.

'Someone has been lying in my bed, too,' said the Mother Bear in her soft mother voice.

'Someone has been lying in my bed and here she is!' cried the Wee Small Bear in his shrill small voice.

Just then Goldilocks awoke. She saw the big furry faces of the three bears looking down at her, and with a loud shriek jumped up and rushed down the stairs and out of the cottage with her hair flying out behind her.

'She is afraid of us!' laughed the Great Rough Bear in his great rough way.

'She is afraid of us!' laughed the Mother Bear in her soft mother way.

'She is afraid of us!' laughed the Wee Small Bear in his wee shrill way.

As for Goldilocks, she didn't stop to draw breath till she was safely home again. And she never again went into a house when she found the door standing open, because for all she knew those three bears might have gobbled her up. How was she to know that they only liked porridge and wild honey?

Jack and the Beanstalk

ONCE upon a time there was a poor widow who had an only son called Jack. All they had in the world was a thin white cow, and at last the day came when the cow had no more milk to give.

'What shall we do? What shall we do?' cried the widow, wringing her hands.

'Perhaps I could go and find work somewhere?' said Jack.

'You? Work? An idle fellow like you?' said his mother. 'We shall need more than that to keep us from starving. No. You'd better take the white cow to market tomorrow and sell her. Then we can use the money to set up a stall in the market, and make our living that way.'

Next morning Jack got up early and set off for market leading the white cow by a rope halter. He was only half way there when he met an old woman all in rags.

'Good morning, Jack,' said she.

'Good morning,' replied Jack, wondering how she knew his name.

'Where are you off to? she asked.

'I'm off to market to sell the cow,' answered Jack.

'You? Sell a cow?' cried the old woman. 'You don't even know how many beans make five!'

'I do, then!' cried Jack. 'Two in each hand and one in your mouth!'

'Right,' nodded she. 'And here are those very beans – all five of them.'

She reached into her pocket and drew out five strange-looking beans, each one of them a different colour.

'I'll give you these beans for your cow,' said she.

Jack shook his head.

'They're magic. If you plant them at night, by morning they'll have grown right up to the sky!'

'Right up to the sky?' cried Jack.

'As ever was,' nodded she. 'And if they don't, you shall have your cow back. Is it a bargain?'

'Done!' said Jack, and he pocketed the five beans and handed over the rope halter to the old woman.

He set off back home, pleased to have made so good a bargain, and glad to have saved himself the trouble of going all the way to market and back. His mother was surprised to see him home again so soon.

'What, back already, Jack?' she said. 'Did you get a good price for the cow?'

'Amazing good,' replied Jack. 'It wasn't money at all I got. Look here at these!'

And he pulled from his pocket the five pretty beans.

'What?' cried his mother. 'What? You've parted with our cow for a handful of beans?'

'They're magic,' said Jack. 'Plant them at night, and in the morning – '

'Dolt!' shrieked his mother, boxing his ears. 'Idiot! Magic indeed! That cow was the last thing we had in the world, and we're ruined now! Ruined!'

She snatched the five beans and threw them right out the window. Then she seized her broom and began to lay about Jack right and left so he ran up the stairs to his room and stayed there all the rest of the day. He didn't dare go down even to fetch food, so he was hungry as well as miserable, and in the end he fell asleep.

When he woke and opened his eyes, he wondered for a minute where he was. It seemed to be neither day nor night, for the room was filled with a strange, greenish glow, as if it were under the sea. Then Jack looked at the window and saw dangling there great green leathery leaves, big as dinner plates, blocking the sky.

'It's those beans!' he cried. 'They've sprouted just like the old woman said!'

He had gone to sleep with his clothes on, so he hopped straight over to the window and looked up and nothing could he see but leaves and thick, twisting branches, up and up and up forever it seemed.

'"Into the sky," she said,' thought Jack. 'Well, then, into the sky I'll go. If I stay here, Mother'll be scolding all day long. Let's see if things look better up there!'

He caught hold of a bough, swung himself out of the window, and began to climb. He climbed and he climbed and he climbed, and after a while he sat astride a branch to rest, and looked back down below. The roof of his own cottage was hidden entirely, but he could see the countryside for miles around, and picked out the steeple at Little Ridding, and Farmer Willow's new barn.

'Not in the sky yet,' he thought, and went on climbing.

He climbed and he climbed and he climbed and next time

he stopped for a rest and looked down below, nothing could he see but thin white cloud, and he knew then that he really was in the sky. Off he went again, and not long after suddenly found there were no more branches above him, and looked round and saw that he was in a strange new country.

There were no trees and flowers as there were at home, only rough grey stones and thing grass, and in the distance what looked like a castle made of rocks.

'We'll see who lives there,' thought Jack.

As he drew near to the castle, a great tall woman, high as a barn door, came on to the doorstep. She had a brown, knobbled face and a pinafore flapping like a ship's sail.

'G-good day,' said Jack politely. 'Could you please give me something to eat? I had no dinner yesterday, nor supper, and I've had no breakfast today, either.'

'It's supper you're wanting, is it?' said the great tall woman. 'It's supper you'll *be* if you don't move off from here sharply. My husband is a

Giant, and if there's one thing he fancies more than another for his supper, it's a boy, grilled on toast!'

Jack stood his ground.

'I may as well be grilled, as die of hunger!' he said. So the Giant's wife let him in, and made him work all day in the kitchen, and in return gave him some supper of a hunk of bread, some cheese and a jug of milk. Just as Jack was finishing his meal there came a great thump-thump-thumping and the whole castle began to tremble.

'Quick!' cried the Giant's wife. 'It's my old man! He'll eat you alive if he finds you here! Into the oven!'

She bundled Jack into the oven and had just slammed the door when in came the Giant, carrying three cows strung from a pole by their heels.

'Boil me a couple of these for supper!' he roared.

Then he began to stride about the kitchen, sniffing mightily, and Jack, crouching in the dark oven, heard his voice growling like thunder:

'Fee Fi Fo Fum
I smell the blood of an Englishman!
Be he alive or be he dead
I'll grind his bones to make my bread!'

'Nonsense, husband!' said his wife. 'It's the beef in the pot you smell. There's no humans about here.'

Jack stayed in the oven while the Giant ate his supper. He could hear his great teeth scrunching the bones, and loud sucking noises as the Giant drank his wine. Then he heard clinking, and peering through a crack, saw two enormous hands counting gold pieces and putting them into leather bags. After that, came snores, great rolling clattering snores like a landslide down a mountain.

Jack crept out of the oven, took the two bags of gold, and ran back down the road to the beanstalk. The bags were so heavy that he had to drop them down, and then he himself scrambled hastily down, to find that they had fallen in his

own garden and burst open, and his mother was hurrying about picking up the pieces.

'Come quick, it's raining gold!' she cried when she saw him.

She was overjoyed to see Jack safely home, and listened to the tale of his adventures in the Giant's castle.

'And now perhaps you'll agree that I made a good bargain for the cow,' said he.

'Oh, I'll agree that,' she said. '*Fifty* cows wouldn't have fetched all this gold.'

For a while the pair of them lived content, but after a time Jack began to wish to visit the Giant's castle again.

'There must be plenty more treasure up there,' he thought. 'And I'm still not so rich as I'd like to be.'

So one day off he set up the beanstalk again, dressed in his fine new clothes, so that the Giant's wife shouldn't recognise him as the raggedy boy who had come before.

Again she let him in and gave him supper, and again she pushed him in the oven when they heard her husband coming.

41

Again the Giant stamped about the kitchen sniffing and bellowing,

'*Fee Fi Fo Fum*
I smell the blood of an Englishman.
Be he alive or be he dead
I'll grind his bones to make my bread!'

'Rubbish, husband!' said his wife. 'You must be getting old! Your nose isn't as sharp as it used to be. It's this roasting elephant you smell, for there's no human flesh about here!'

The Giant ate his supper, and then roared to his wife,

'Fetch the hen that lays the golden eggs!'

Jack put his eye to the crack again and saw her put a fine brown hen on the table before him.

'Lay!' roared the Giant. And sure enough, the hen laid a bright golden egg that shone in the firelight, and had no sooner done so than her master again cried 'Lay!' and she laid another, then another, then another.

When he was tired of the game, the Giant put all the golden eggs into a bag, put his head on the table, and began to snore fit to bring the ceiling down.

Jack crept out of the oven and tucked the hen under his arm and was nearly out at the door when the hen let out a loud cackle. The Giant stirred in his sleep, and muttered,

'Wife, what are you doing to my hen?'

Jack didn't wait to hear an answer to *that* question. He ran and ran till he reached the beanstalk, then climbed down and down till he was safely home again.

He showed his mother the hen, and after that whenever he cried 'Lay!' the brown hen would lay an egg of purest gold.

Time went by, and again Jack began to feel restless.

'I must go back just one more time,' he said to himself – he dared not say it to his mother, for she would never have agreed. After all, they had only to say the word 'lay!' and they had gold enough to last them a year, so why should they complain?

One morning Jack climbed out of his window early so as not to rouse his mother, and set off again up the long green road into the sky. This time he dared not knock at the castle door for fear the Giant's wife would know him. So he waited till she was out in the yard, pegging out handkerchiefs big enough for bed linen, and then crept into the kitchen. This time, he hid inside the copper, instead of the oven.

As soon as the Giant returned he began to sniff and stride about the kitchen, shouting,

'Fee Fi Fo Fum
I smell the blood of an Englishman!
Be he alive or be he dead
I'll grind his bones to make my bread!'

'You must be mistaken, husband,' said the Giant's wife. 'There's no humans here. And better not be! Creeping up and stealing all your gold and your magic hen! If there's any human here, I'll mince him up and make a stew of him, or a nice meat pattie!'

She flung open the oven door as she spoke, and Jack shivered and shook inside the copper and began to wish he had never come. At last, they gave up looking and sat down to their meal of a roast pig each and a tureen of soup you could have drowned a man in.

When he had finished, the Giant pushed away his plate and roared,

'Fetch me my golden harp, wife, and we'll have some music to play us to sleep!'

So the wife went out and came back with a great golden harp that shone so brightly that it lit up the whole room.

'Play!' commanded the Giant. And the harp began to play of its own accord sweet music, golden as its own strings, till both the Giant and his wife laid their heads on the table and went to sleep.

Carefully Jack raised the lid of the copper and climbed out. He crept slowly towards the table, seeing the Giants' boots before him, big as cottages. Then, very gently, he lifted the harp and went tip-toe to the door. But just as he reached it, the harp called out loudly,

'Master! Master!'

The Giant woke with a start just in time to see Jack disappear round the door with the glittering harp tucked under his arm.

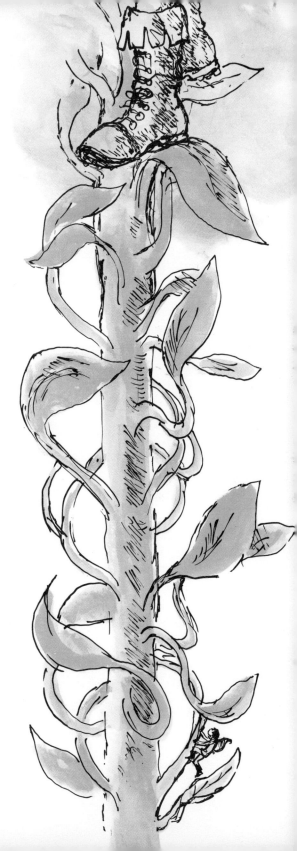

'Robbers! Thieves!' roared the Giant. 'Wife, wake up!'

Jack ran as he had never run before, feeling the ground tremble under his feet as the two giants came chasing after him.

He swung himself on to the beanstalk and down he went, hand over hand, safe again, as he thought. But he had barely gone half way when the beanstalk began to shake and sway. and looking up, Jack to his horror far away above him, a pair of enormous boots! The Giant was coming down after him!

'Mother! Mother!' Jack was below the clouds now, and from the corner of his eye could see the spire and Farmer Willow's barn. 'Mother, mother! Fetch the axe!'

The beanstalk swayed and leaned and shook.

'Mother! Mother, fetch the axe!'

Far away down below Jack's mother, fetched outdoors by the wild shaking of the leaves outside her window, ran for the axe and stood ready at the bottom of the beanstalk.

As Jack reached the ground

45

he thrust the golden harp into his mother's hands, snatched the axe and began to lay into the stem of the beanstalk, crash, crash, crash!

The stem was still young and juicy, and at the seventh stroke of the axe it began to split. The stalk gave a last, circling shudder, there was a mighty yell from above and then the whole beanstalk from earth to sky, all the long green length of it, leaned – and toppled. There was a thud as the giant hit the ground in the next field, a last shaking of leaves, and then silence.

Jack and his mother stared and saw the beanstalk lying before them like a thick green rope right away on and on out of sight and into the next shire for all they knew. Then they turned about and went indoors and ate their supper and played the golden harp. And what with the harp and the hen that laid golden eggs they were rich and happy from that day forth, and as for Jack, he married a princess – and deserved to.

Snow White and the Seven Dwarfs

A QUEEN sat sewing by the window one day when the snow was falling. She lifted her head to see a raven walking on the white lawns, and as she did so, pricked her finger. A drop of blood fell, and in that moment the Queen made a wish.

'I wish that I might have a little daughter, and that her skin might be as white as snow, her lips red as blood and her hair black as a raven's wing.'

She spoke the wish out loud and when she had finished the raven spread his black wings and flew off into the swirling snow.

Not long afterwards a daughter was born to the King and Queen, and the Queen, remembering her wish, called the child Snow White. And as she grew older her skin was white as snow, her lips were red as blood and her hair shone like a raven's wing.

After a few years the Queen died and the King married again. His new wife was beautiful and proud. She would gaze and gaze at herself in a magic glass that hung in her room, and say to it,

'*Mirror, Mirror on the wall,*
Who is the fairest of us all?'
Then the glass would answer,
'*Pale as the moon, bright as a star,*
Thou art the fairest, Queen, by far!'

And the Queen would smile at her reflection in the cold glass and stretch her neck like a swan and preen.

But Snow White grew more and more beautiful each day, and when she was seven years old she was even fairer than the Queen herself.

The magic mirror could not tell a lie, and so when next the Queen asked it,

'*Mirror, Mirror on the wall,*
Who is the fairest of us all?'

the reply came,

'*Fair as the day, O Queen, you are,*
But Snow White is lovelier by far!'

At this the Queen turned white with rage. She sent for a huntsman and told him to take Snow White deep into the forest and there to kill her. But when the huntsman drew his knife to plunge it into her heart, and Snow White began to cry and beg for her life, he remembered his own children at home, and slowly let the knife fall.

'Run as far off as you can,' he told her. 'If ever you return, we shall both lose our lives.'

Then he turned and left her, and on his way back to the palace he killed a fawn and cut out its heart to take back to the Queen, pretending it was Snow White's.

Now Snow White was alone in the dim green forest and as she ran the brambles clutched at her dress like live hands and the sharp stones cut into her feet. But the wild animals that roamed by let her pass without harming her, and she ran and ran all day until it was evening. Then, in the dusk, she came upon a little house, the first she had seen all day, and because she was so tired, went inside to rest.

Inside, everything was very small and yet neat and clean as could be. There was a small table set out with a white cloth and seven little plates and seven little loaves and seven little glasses with wine in them. By the wall were seven little beds, neatly made with not a wrinkle in the counterpanes.

Snow White was so hungry that she went right round the table taking a little nibble of each loaf, a forkful of vegetables from each plate and a sip of wine from each glass.

Then, because she was so tired after her day in the forest, she went to the row of beds and tried first one and then another

till she found the most comfortable. She lay down and went straight to sleep.

Soon afterwards, the owners of the house came home. They were seven dwarfs, who worked all day deep in the mountainside with pick and shovel, digging for gold and precious stones. In they came and took off their boots and left them in a row by the door. Then they lit the lamps and saw at once that things were not as they had left them.

'Who has been sitting in my chair?' said the first.

'Who has been using my fork?' said the second.

'Who has been nibbling my bread?' said the third.

'Who has been picking at my vegetables?' said the fourth.

'Who has been drinking out of my glass?' said the fifth.

'Who has been cutting with my knife?' said the sixth.

'And who has been eating off my plate?' said the seventh.

Then one of them went over to his bed and saw a dent in the counterpane and he cried,

'Someone has been sitting on my bed!'

Then all the rest ran up to their beds crying, 'And mine! And mine!' until the seventh dwarf went to *his* bed and found Snow White herself, fast asleep.

'Sssssh!' he hissed loudly to the others. 'Sssh! Come and look!'

All seven dwarfs crowded round the bed whispering and nudging one another and all fixing their eyes on Snow White's beautiful face.

'What a lovely child!' they whispered. 'We mustn't wake her!'

So all through the night the seven dwarfs took turns to watch by Snow White's bedside, an hour each until morning

came. When she awoke and saw the seven dwarfs Snow White
was frightened and covered her eyes. But they spoke gently
to her and asked her name and how she had come there alone
through the thick forest. Snow White told them her story,
and when she had finished the first dwarf asked,

'Can you cook and sew and spin? Can you dust and sweep
and kindle fires? Can you knit and bake and can you trim a
lamp?'

Snow White could do all these things, because her stepmother had kept her hard at work at home. And so the dwarfs
said that she could stay with them and look after the house
while they went off each day to dig for gold and silver in the
mountains.

Each day, before they set off in the grey dawn the dwarfs
would warn Snow White,

'Take care to let no one in. One day the Queen will find out
where you are and try to harm you.'

All this time the Queen had thought Snow White was dead,
and was so sure that she was now the most beautiful in the land
that she had not troubled to use her magic glass. But one day,

when she had nothing else to do, she went and sat before it, smiled at her reflection and asked,

'*Mirror, Mirror on the wall,*
Who is the fairest of us all?'

And the glass answered,

'*Queen, thou art fairest here, I hold,*
But in the forest and over fell
Snow White with the seven dwarfs doth dwell
And she is fairer, a thousandfold!'

At this the Queen was mad with hate and envy, and lifted her arm to shatter the mirror into a thousand pieces. But her arm fell, and she thought,

'No. It is not the mirror I must destroy, but Snow White!'

Next day she stained her face brown and dressed in rags like a pedlar woman and set off into the forest to the cottage of the seven dwarfs. There she stood beneath the window with her big hat shading her face and called out,

'Wares to sell! Wares to sell!'

Snow White put her head out of the window.

'Good day,' she said. 'What have you to sell?'

'Pretty trinkets,' replied the wicked Queen. 'And coloured laces for your waist!'

She held up one of plaited scarlet silk, dangling it under Snow White's eyes so that she thought,

'Surely I may let this pedlar in? She seems kind and honest, and has such pretty things!'

She opened the door and the Queen went in.

'Gracious, child!' she cried. 'How badly your dress is laced! Here, let *me* do it, with this pretty scarlet lace, and you shall have it for a penny!'

Snow White stood quite still while the pedlar threaded the new red lace with nimble fingers. But the wicked Queen pulled the laces tighter and tighter and tighter till at last all the breath was squeezed out of Snow White's body and she fell to the floor and lay there as if she were dead.

'That's the end of *you* and your beauty!' cried the spiteful Queen, and hastened back towards the palace.

When the dwarfs came back and found Snow White lying lifeless on the floor they guessed at once what had happened. One of them seized a knife and cut the scarlet lace and at once Snow White drew in a great sigh and began to breathe again. The dwarfs gave a shout of joy, and next day when they set off in the mists for the mountains they begged her to take care, and be on the watch for the wicked Queen.

That very morning the Queen herself rose early and went to the magic mirror.

'*Mirror, mirror on the wall*
Who is the fairest of us all?'

When the mirror gave the same answer as before the Queen could not speak for anger. In terrible silence she dressed in a disguise, a different one, and took up a tray of gay combs and painted one of them with deadly poison. She set off to the

dwarfs' house and there she knocked on the door and cried,
'Fine wares to sell! Fine wares to sell!'

Again Snow White looked through the window, and said,
'I cannot open the door – I dare not! I have promised to
let no-one in!'

'There is no need to open the door,' replied the Queen.
'Just look at my beautiful combs. See, I will pass one up for
you to try.'

She picked out a carved comb of finest ivory. Snow White
took it from her and put it into her hair and no sooner had
she done so than she fell to the floor in a deadly swoon.

'There you may lie!' cried the wicked Queen, and went her
way.

Luckily, that day the dwarfs came home from the mountains
early and found Snow White before she was quite dead. They
gently took the poisoned comb from her hair and after a time
she opened her eyes and sat up. When she told them what had
happened they warned her yet again to beware, and again
Snow White promised that she would.

That very night the Queen went to her magic mirror again. When she received the same reply as before and knew that Snow White must still be living she shivered and shook from head to foot with rage. She pointed her long white finger into the mirror and it pointed back at her.

'Snow White shall die!' she cried. 'Even if it cost *my* life!'

All night long she secretly worked at a poisoned apple. One side of it was rosy and shining, the other clear and green. Whoever took a bite from the red side was sure to die.

At dawn the Queen went gliding out to the woods dressed as a peasant's wife. When she came to the dwarfs' house she knocked and Snow White put her head out of the window.

'I cannot open the door,' she said. 'The dwarfs have told me not to.'

'Very well,' said the old woman. 'It doesn't matter to me whether you do or not. But perhaps you'd like this pretty apple as a present before I go?'

Snow White shook her head.

'What is the matter?' asked the peasant woman. 'Do you think that it is poisoned? Silly girl – see, watch me!'

She turned the green side of the apple to her lips and bit into it.

'There!' said she. 'If it were poisoned, do you think *I* should have eaten it? Here, take the rest and eat it!'

Snow White longed for the shining red apple with its juicy flesh. She took it from the old woman, bit into the rosy skin and next minute fell to the ground.

'This time nothing shall save her!' cried the Queen, and hastened back to the castle. There she went and stood before the magic mirror and at last it gave her the answer she wanted,

'*Thou art the fairest, Queen, by far!*'

When the dwarfs came home, laden with gold in the twilight, they found Snow White lying there and lifted her up and splashed her face with cold water and did everything they could think of to bring her back to life. It was in vain. Snow

White's eyelids never flickered, not the faintest breath floated from her lips. For seven days and seven nights they watched by her side, but there was not the least stir of life. For all that, Snow White was still so beautiful that they could hardly bring themselves to believe that she was really dead.

'We can't bury her in the cold ground!' they cried. And they made a coffin of glass and placed her in it and wrote her name on it in gold letters. They carried the coffin to the hillside and one of the dwarfs always sat by it and watched, day and night. And all the birds of the air came singly out of the sky to lament the death of Snow White, the owl, the raven, and at last the dove.

Snow White lay many years on the bare mountain side and still she seemed only to sleep. Her lips were red as blood, her skin was white as snow and her hair black as a raven's wing just as they had been in life.

It happened one day that the son of a king came riding by and saw Snow White within her glass walls. He read the gold lettering and learned her name, and that she was the daughter of a king.

'Give her to me!' he begged the dwarfs. But they all shook
their heads and refused to let her go.

'I will give you gold and treasure,' pleaded the Prince.

Again they refused.

'We will not give her up for all the treasure in the world!'

'Then I shall stay here on the mountain all my days looking
on Snow White', said the Prince. 'I cannot live without her'.

At this, the dwarfs pitied him and could not deny him what
he asked. They themselves helped to lift the coffin, and as
they did so, the piece of poisoned apple fell from Snow
White's lips. She opened her eyes, lifted her head, and cried
in astonishment,

'What is happening?'

The Prince, overjoyed, lifted her from the coffin and told
her the story of how she had been poisoned by the wicked
Queen and had lain like one dead for more than seven years.

'But now you have come to life again,' he said. 'And I love

you better than all the world. Come with me to my father's kingdom and marry me!'

And so Snow White said farewell to the seven dwarfs and went with the Prince to his father's castle where a great feast was prepared for their wedding. Among the guests invited was Snow White's wicked stepmother. She dressed herself in her finest clothes and when she was ready, stood before the magic glass and smiled proudly.

'*Mirror, mirror on the wall,*
Who is the fairest of us all?'
And the glass replied,
'*Fair as the day, O Queen, you are,*
But the new bride is lovelier, by far!'

At this the Queen's fury was so great that she lifted her jewelled hand and struck the glass and it broke into a thousand pieces. Then she went out and rode to the wedding, so that she could see with her own eyes this bride who was even more beautiful than herself.

And when she went into the hall and saw that the bride was none other than Snow White, she flew into such a passion of hate and envy that her heart burst and she fell down dead.

But Snow White and the Prince were married that day and lived and reigned happily ever after.

The Frog Prince

ONE evening a young princess went into a wood and sat down under a lime tree by a spring of clear water. She had taken with her her favourite plaything, a beautiful golden ball, and kept tossing it idly into the air and catching it again.

Each time she threw it higher and higher, until at last she threw it too high and too far, and missed catching it as it fell. It began to roll away from her, away and away, and before she could run after it, rolled right into the spring itself.

'My ball! O, my ball!' cried the Princess in dismay.

She went and craned right over the edge of the well, but the water was very deep and she knew that she could never reach to the bottom of it. She began to cry, because she had really loved her golden ball, and could not bear to think that she would never play with it again.

'I loved it best of everything in the whole world,' she sobbed. 'And I'd give anything – everything I've got, to have it back again. All my jewels, all my fine clothes – everything!'

As she finished speaking a frog suddenly put its flat green head out of the water and asked,

'Princess, why do you weep so bitterly?.

'O frog, I have lost my golden ball!' she cried. 'It has fallen into the spring and now I shall never see it again!'

'You *may* see it again,' replied the frog, 'if you let me help you. I heard what you said just now. I do not want your jewels or your fine clothes. But if you will love me, and let me live with you, and eat from your little golden plate and sleep upon your bed, then I will bring you back your ball again.'

He sat with his green head cocked and looked at the Princess with his great round eyes, and she looked back at him.

'What nonsense he talks!' thought the Princess. 'How could he possibly climb out of the well? And as for coming to live with me at the palace – it's impossible! But he may be able to dive down and fetch my pretty ball, so I'll pretend to promise what he asks.'

'Very well, frog,' she said out loud. 'I will agree to what you ask. And now – dive and fetch me my ball quickly – do!'

So the frog splashed down into the water and disappeared. Next minute he came up again with the ball in his mouth and tossed it to the ground at the Princess's feet.

'O thank you!' cried the Princess, overjoyed. 'My ball – my beautiful ball!'

She picked it up and ran gaily off towards the palace, quite forgetting the frog and her own promise.

'Princess, wait!' called the frog after her. 'Remember what you promised!'

But the Princess kept on running, and soon was safely home again, her adventure forgotten.

Next day, the Princess was just sitting down to her dinner when there came a strange, soft pattering noise as if slippered feet were coming up the marble staircase. Sure enough, next moment there came a gentle knocking at the door, and a voice said:

'*Open the door, my Princess dear,*
Open the door to thy true love here!
Remember the words the two of us said
By the fountain cool in the greenwood shade!'

The Princess ran to the door and opened it, and there stood the frog, whom she had quite forgotten! The sight of him frightened her so much that she slammed the door shut again in his face and hurried back to her seat. The King himself was sitting at the table.

'Who was that at the door?' he asked.

'Only a nasty frog,' replied the Princess. 'My golden ball fell into the spring yesterday, and he fetched it out for me. But he made me make a silly promise, to let him come here and live with me, and now he's wanting to be let in!'

As she was speaking the frog was knocking at the door again, and saying his sad little song:

'*Open the door, my Princess dear,*
Open the door to thy true love here!
Remember the words the two of us said
By the fountain cool in the greenwood shade!'

'You must let him in,' said the King. 'If you made a promise, you must keep it. Open the door.'

Much against her will the Princess went and opened the door, and the frog came hopping in and went right over to the table.

'I am hungry,' he said to the Princess. 'Pray lift me on to a chair, so that I may sit by you.'

She did as he asked, though she could hardly bear to touch him, and when she herself had sat down again, he said,

'Push your plate a little closer to me, so that I may eat out of it.'

The Princess was forced to obey, though she did not at all like the idea of sharing her plate with a frog.

When he had eaten as much as he could, the frog said,

'Now I am tired. Pray carry me upstairs and put me on your own little bed.'

The Princess was bound by her promise to do as he asked. She picked up the frog very gingerly, between her fingers,

carried him upstairs, and with a shudder dropped him on to her own bed. He crept up on to the pillow, and there he slept all night long. But when morning came, he jumped up and hopped down the stairs and out of the palace.

'Thank heaven!' cried the Princess. 'Now he has gone, and I shall see no more of him!'.

But she was mistaken. That night as she sat at table there came again that same soft slippery footstep on the stair, and that same gentle knocking at the door. Once again the Princess was forced to feed the frog from her own golden plate, and take him up to her own bed to sleep.

On the third night, when again the frog visited her, the Princess began to regret her promise bitterly.

But on the third morning when she woke, it was to find the frog gone already from her pillow. And there, standing at the foot of the bed, was the most handsome prince she had ever seen, gazing at her with eyes that were loving and gentle and strangely like those of the little frog.

'Dear Princess!' cried the Prince then. 'You have broken the spell at last!'

He told her how he had been enchanted by a wicked fairy. She had changed him into a frog, and told him that he would never again take human shape unless he could find a Princess who would take him from the spring and bring him home with her, to feed from her own plate and sleep upon her bed.

'And now you have done this,' cried the Prince, 'and I love you dearly, and want you to come with me to my own kingdom and marry me, and be my queen.'

And so it happened. Next day the Princess drove off with her Prince in a fine golden coach drawn by six white horses, bound for his own kingdom, where they married and lived happily ever after.

Rumpelstiltskin

ONCE upon a time there lived a poor miller who had a very beautiful daughter. One day this man had to go and speak with the king. He dressed in his best clothes but still he felt even poorer and humbler than usual as he walked through the high palace gates. So when he was face to face with the king, to make himself seem more important and a man of the world, he told the king in an offhand way,

'I have a daughter who can spin straw into gold!'

The King was very interested indeed to hear this.

'Well, Miller,' said he, '*that* is something I have never heard of before. Bring your daughter to the palace tomorrow, and we will see what she can do.'

The miller could have bitten out his tongue. Why ever had he told such a ridiculous tale? For, of course, his daughter could *not* spin straw into gold. If she had been able, he himself would not have been living in a tumbledown mill with idle sails.

When he went home he told his daughter what had happened, and the poor girl wondered whatever her fate would be when the truth was discovered? But next day she put a brave face upon it, and she too dressed in her best clothes and went to the palace.

The King greeted her kindly and then took her to a room that was filled with straw. The only other things in the room were a spinning wheel and stool.

'Now you can get to work,' he told her. 'And if by morning you have not turned all the straw into gold, then you must die.'

The door closed and the key turned in the lock. The miller's daughter stared round at the tumbled yellow straw and heartily wished herself safe back home at the draughty mill. She knew that she could sit there for a year, let alone a night, and still the straw would be nothing but straw. At last, because there was nothing to do but wait for the morning when she must die, the miller's daughter began to weep.

After a time the door opened, and in came a strange little brown-faced man.

'Good-day,' said he, doffing his cap, 'Why are you crying, miller's daughter?'

'Because I must spin this straw into gold before morning, or else I shall die!'

'What will you give me if *I* spin the straw?' asked the queer little man. He was wrinkled and bearded and no higher than her knee.

'I would give you anything in the world!' she cried, 'But I have only my necklace!'

He nodded sharply and held out his hand.

'That will do,' he said. The miller's daughter gave him the necklace and he seated himself at the spinning wheel and whirr, whirr, whirr – three turns and the reel was full of gold

thread. He put another in, and whirr, whirr, whirr – that was full too. All night long the miller's daughter watched till she was dizzy, seeing the long yellow straws magically spun into finest gold thread. When the last reel was filled, the little man bowed and doffed his cap and was gone without a word.

At break of day the King himself came in, and when he found the straw gone and the reels filled with spun gold he was beside himself with delight and wonder. But the sight of so much treasure made him more greedy than ever, and instead of rewarding the miller's daughter, he took her to another, even larger room, filled with straw, and commanded her to spin it into gold by morning or else die.

Again the miller's daughter sat and wept and again the door opened and the strange mannikin appeared.

'What will you give me this time if I do the work?' he asked her.

'The very last thing I have in the world now,' she replied. 'My ring.'

She took it from her finger and gave it to him, and the little man sat down straightway to spin. By morning the task was done and he went away just before the King himself came in.

The King was again delighted, and later that day he took the miller's daughter to a third room, still larger than the others. But this time he said to her,

'If you can spin this straw to gold by morning you shall be my wife!'

As soon as she was left alone the little man appeared, and as before, asked, 'What will you give me if I spin the straw this time?'

'Alas!' she cried, 'I have nothing left to give you!'

'If I *do* spin the straw,' said he, 'then you will become Queen. Promise me that if you do, you will give me your first child!'

The miller's daughter was forced to agree, and because she had spent two sleepless nights, fell asleep to the soft humming

of the wheel. When she awoke it was dawn and the room
gleamed with a faint golden light. As she rubbed her eyes and
stared at the stacks of glittering gold the King entered and
saw that the work was done.

'Now you shall become my Queen,' he told her, 'and
never more spin straw to gold.'

For he had enough treasure now to last him for the rest of
his days.

And so they married and lived happily together for a year,
when the Queen had a beautiful child. By now she had quite
forgotten her promise to the little man. But one day he suddenly appeared before her as she sat embroidering, and said,

'Now you must give me what you promised!'

The Queen was horrified, and offered him all the riches of
her kingdom if he would only leave her the child. Sharply he
shook his head.

'What are riches to me?' he said. 'I can spin gold from
straw. But something that is living is dearer to me than all the
treasures in the world!'

The Queen, broken-hearted, began to cry. The little man stood and frowned and fidgeted, and at last he said gruffly,

'Very well. I will give you three days' time. If by then you can find out my name, then I will let you keep your child, and trouble you no more.'

With these words he left, and straightway the Queen summoned a messenger and sent him out to find the names of all the people living in the neighbourhood. When the little man came back next day, she read out a whole list of names to him.

'Roderick?'

'No.'

'Caspar?'

'No.'

'Benjamin?'

'No.'

And so on right down the list.

Next day, the Queen sent out another messenger and this time gave orders that he was to find out as many odd and unusual names as he could. When the little man appeared before her for the second time, she began her list. None of the names were very likely ones – but then he was not a very likely little man, either.

'Perhaps your name is Sheepshanks or Needlenob or Lippetylegs?' she began.

The mannikin shook his head till his beard swung. The Queen went on with her list – Nobblenose, Pennyweather, Bullybags and Snout, but at every single name the little man shook his head. The Queen was in despair.

Then, on the third day, just before evening, a messenger came back with a strange tale.

'I was riding in the woods,' he told her, 'when I came to a small hut in a clearing. A fire was burning outside the house, and round it capered the queerest little fellow I ever sat eyes on. And as he danced, he was shouting this song,

> *'Merrily the feast I'll make,*
> *Today I'll brew, tomorrow bake.*
> *Merrily I'll dance and sing*
> *Tomorrow will a stranger bring.*
> *Little does my lady dream*
> *Rumpelstiltskin is my name!'*

When she heard this the Queen was overjoyed. When the little man came, his eyes glowing as he looked at the baby in his cradle, she began by asking quite ordinary names. At each of them he shook his head and his eyes glittered the more. Then, at last, the Queen drew a deep breath and,

'Can Rumpelstiltskin be your name?'

The little man let out a scream of fury.

'A witch has told you that! A witch has told you that!' he screamed, and he stamped his right foot so hard that it went right down through the floor! He had to get hold of it and pull and tug with both hands to get it out again, and when it *did* come out he fell right over, and the Queen and her court rocked with laughter. Then he went hobbling off as best he could, and Rumpelstiltskin was never heard of again.

The Ugly Duckling

IT was summertime in the country. The wheat was yellow, the oats were green and the hay stood in stacks. An old manor house basked in the sun, surrounded by a moat where the burdocks grew so high that the children could stand right up under their leaves. And hidden in the long grass by the moat was a mother duck, hatching out her eggs.

At first it had been pleasant enough to sit in the sun and watch the world go by, but by now she was thoroughly bored by the whole business. Luckily, the eggs were about to hatch, and one after another they cracked open and little wet heads poked out.

'Quack!' said the mother duck, pleased. 'Quack! Quick! Quick!'

And they *were* quick – all except one. One particularly large egg showed not a sign of hatching. It lay smooth and blank without so much as a crack, while the little hatched-out ducklings cheeped and scrambled around it, staring curiously at the great green world about them.

'What's the *matter* with this egg?' grumbled the mother duck, who could hardly wait to take her brood down to the water.

'It's a *big* one,' said an old duck who had come to visit. 'It looks like a turkey egg to me. You'll have trouble if it is. Turkeys can't swim!'

At last, the egg *did* hatch, and out scrambled a big, grey ugly chick on clumsy feet. The duck looked at him.

'What an ugly looking creature!' she said. 'Not a bit like the others. But turkey or not, he'll go in the water with the rest even if I have to *kick* him in!'

She waddled down to the moat, followed by her brood. Splash! Splash! In they went, and before the duck had time to turn her head splash! in went the big grey one, swimming beautifully, with his head held high and big feet paddling strongly under the water.

'Well!' exclaimed the duck, pleased. 'He may be ugly, but he's not so bad, after all. See how he swims!!'

They spent the morning floating under the green shade of the burdocks and then the duck took them down to the farmyard.

'Mind your manners and watch out for the cat,' she told them. 'Keep your toes turned out when you walk as I do, and bow nicely when you're spoken to!'

The farmyard was full of ducks and hens and turkeys and they all gathered round to stare at the new arrivals.

'What's that you've got there?' asked one duck. '*That's* no duckling! Great ugly thing! Get him out of here!'

She flew at the ugly duckling and bit him in the neck. The duckling's mother ruffled her feathers.

'Let him alone!' she said. 'He's doing no harm!'

But the poor duckling could do nothing right in the farm-yard. The ducks and hens jostled and pushed him and gave him a sharp peck when his mother was not looking. Whenever he tried to pick about for corn they shoo'd him away, and one old turkey cock flew at him like a ship in full sail, gobbling and scolding till his face was crimson.

The days that followed were even worse. The duckling's own brothers and sisters turned against him too, and made fun of him because his feet were so clumsy and his neck was long and lop-sided.

'Why don't you go away, you ugly thing?' they said. Even the poultry maid who came out with the corn kicked out at him whenever she saw him near. His own mother grew tired of him, and would say,

'How I wish you'd never hatched out – I'm thoroughly ashamed of you. Why don't you go away?'

And so, one day, the ugly duckling did go away. He could bear it no longer. He flew over the hedge and out over the open fields and on and on far away from the farmyard till he came at dusk to the great marshes where the wild ducks lived. There he crept among the rushes and fell asleep.

Next morning the wild ducks crowded round, staring and jeering.

'*You're* an ugly object!' they said. 'Whatever are you?'

The duckling got to his feet and bowed to them as best he could, as his mother had taught him. But instead of bowing back, or at least nodding their heads, the ducks and geese let out loud, piercing shrieks of laughter and raced up into the air with a beating of wings.

Bang! Bang! Shots rang out over the quiet marsh and two ganders fell dead among the rushes while the water ran blood red. Bang! Bang! Blue smoke drifted in wisps over the grey water. The ugly duckling lay trembling among the rushes, seeing the other birds fall like stones. Then he heard voices shouting and saw men with guns rise to their feet in the distance and next minute an enormous dog with tongue lolling thrust its head right down over the little duckling. For a moment its jaws opened, horribly wide and edged with sharp teeth, and then – splash, it had gone, and the duckling opened his eyes again.

'Even the *dog* doesn't fancy me,' he thought miserably. 'I must be the ugliest creature that ever was born!'

All day the guns cracked and the dogs barked about him. Then, towards evening, when everything was still again, the duckling plucked up courage to come out of his hiding place in the reeds. He cocked his head, heard nothing, and began to scamper off away from the marshes as fast as his legs could carry him.

At nightfall he came to a little tumbledown house and there he crept in through a broken board and slept till morning. In this house lived an old woman with her cat and her hen. The cat was called Sonny and could arch its back and purr, and if you stroked its fur the wrong way it could make sparks fly. The hen was called Chickabiddy Dumpy because it had such short little legs, and the woman loved it as if it were her own child.

They were all very surprised to find the strange duckling there in the morning, and the old woman, who was very short sighted, thought he was a duck.

'What a find!' she said. 'Now I shall have duck's eggs for breakfast. I'll keep it for a while, and see what happens.'

But, of course, the ugly duckling could *not* lay eggs, and soon he was being scolded and made fun of as much as before.

'A fine creature you are!' the cat would say, arching his back. 'Can you purr?'

'No.'

'Can you make sparks fly?'

'No.'

'*What* a creature!' and the cat would go winding about the old woman's legs purring till he was given milk.

One day, the duckling sat in a corner of the hut and all at once remembered the fresh air and the sunshine. He remembered how he had flown free over hedges and fields, and best of all, how happily he had sailed over the green waters of the moat. So great was his longing that he could not keep it to himself, and he told the hen about it. She drew herself into her feathers and fixed him with a disapproving eye.

'Water?' she cackled. 'Sky? What are you talking about? Isn't life good enough for you here? Aren't you grateful to us for taking you in, ugly creature that you are, and feeding you, and giving you a home?'

The duckling was silent. He was seeing in his mind's eye the wide green meadows and the far off silver curve of a river.

'Ungrateful creature!' went on the hen. 'Can you purr? Can you lay eggs?'

'No,' said the duckling.

'Well, then,' said the hen. 'When you can make yourself useful, *that* will be the time to talk. Sky indeed! Water indeed! Whoever heard such rubbish!'

'But I long to go out into the wide world!' cried the ugly duckling.

'Well then, go!' snapped the hen.

So the duckling went. And though he had not a friend in the world because of his ugliness, at least he had the whole wide sky to roam and the deep waters of the lakes and rivers to sail.

Autumn came. The leaves turned sere and yellow. The skies darkened and the air was chill and misty. The duckling shivered at the thought of the winter to come.

One evening as he looked for a place to sleep, he heard long, strange cries, and looking up, saw a flock of great birds flying out of the crimson sunset. The duckling felt his feathers stir with delight and wonder. He had never in his life seen anything so beautiful. Their wings were gleaming white and their long necks reached forward and they uttered long, hungry cries as they beat steadily through the air – high, so high that the little duckling grew dizzy looking up at them. He himself spun round on the water like a wheel, turning his head to look after them, and his neck stretched and strained and he too let out a hoarse, loud cry.

Then they were gone. The duckling crept into the rushes, put his head under his wing, and dreamed of the beautiful white birds. After that, every day he thought of them, and longed to see them again.

The winter was bitterly cold. The duckling searched from morning to night for food, and when he was on the water he had to paddle his feet the whole time to keep the water from freezing up about him. Each day the frost deepened, the ice thickened, until at last the time came when the duckling grew faint and dizzy as he paddled, and lay quite still, and froze fast in the ice.

Early next morning a farmer came by and saw him. He broke the ice, lifted the duckling out and took him home to his wife. There he slowly revived, and when he lifted his head and rose to his feet the children rushed at him, wanting to play.

But the ugly duckling thought they wished to harm him and flew up in a panic, upsetting a pail and sending the milk all over the room. The woman screamed and waved her arms and the duckling, more frightened than ever, flew into the butter tub, and then into the flour bin in a shower of white. The children shouted with laughter and the duckling, terrified, dived past them out through the open door and into the bushes. There he lay for a long time, dazed and trembling.

But the winter was nearly over now. One day as the duckling lay on the marsh among the rushes, a pale sun broke through the clouds and all at once the larks began to sing. Spring was coming!

The duckling lifted and spread his wings and before he knew it was up in the air under the warm sun. On and on he flew, not knowing where he was going, until at last he alighted in a beautiful garden full of apple blossom and sweet smelling lilac.

Under the trailing boughs of the willow on the clear water of the lake came three beautiful white swans. The duckling knew them at once. He had dreamed of them all the winter long.

'I must go to them,' he thought. 'What if they do peck me to death? What do I care? Better that than spend the rest of my life being pecked and kicked and scolded, and without a single friend.'

And so he boldly slipped into the water and swam towards the splendid birds. They ruffled their white feathers as they came to meet him, and as he drew near the duckling bowed his head, waiting for them to attack him.

But nothing happened. And stranger still, as he rode smoothly on the lake, the water settled and grew calm about him and in its depth he saw another beautiful white bird with graceful neck and snowy feathers.

He bowed his head to it, and the bird bowed back, and all at once he saw that it was himself, it was his own reflection! Gone was the clumsy, grey-black duckling with its ragged feathers and hanging head. There instead was a royal swan with smooth plumage and proud head on a long, curving neck.

The ugly duckling had turned into a swan!

Then the other swans swam round him and stroked him with their beaks, welcoming him because he was one of them, and beautiful. And the children playing in the park ran down to the lake crying,

'Look! Look! A new swan? Isn't he beautiful? The most beautiful of all!'

They threw crusts and crumbs and the new swan dipped for them with his beak. The sun shone, the lilac hung in clusters over his head, his brother swans swam by his side. Never in all his life had he dreamed that there could be so much happiness in the world.

'I am a swan,' he said to himself. He had to keep saying it, all day long. 'I was an ugly duckling, and now I have turned into a swan!'

Cinderella

THERE was once a man whose first wife had died, and so he married again. He did not pick so well the second time. His new wife was spiteful and bad-tempered and to make matters worse, she had two daughters who both took after her.

This man already had a daughter, and she was kind and gentle and beautiful. So the step-mother and her daughters were thoroughly jealous of her, and soon set about making her life as miserable as they could.

They gave her all the dirty work in the house. She scrubbed and scoured and dusted all day long while her new sisters lay polishing their nails or prinking themselves in the glass. They wore jewels and silks and satins while their poor sister had only a few rags to her back. They slept on soft feather mattresses, deep and warm, while she shivered on straw in the draughty attic.

And she patiently worked and shivered and half-starved without saying a single word of complaint to her father.

At the end of the day when all the work was done, she would sit huddled among the cinders in the chimney corner of the kitchen, trying to keep warm. Even this did not make the ugly sisters sorry. Instead, they laughed, and gave her the nickname of Cinderella.

One day, the king of all the land gave a great ball for his son, the prince. The step-mother and her daughters were invited, and were soon busily planning what they would wear and how they would dress their hair.

While the two ugly sisters posed before the glasses, trying out sashes and twirling their hair into ringlets, Cinderella was sent rushing hither and thither to fetch and carry, to sew and

press, so that everything would be ready on the night of the ball. Instead of being grateful for her help, the two sisters mocked her.

'How would you like to go to the ball, Cinderella?' they asked.

'Oh, I would!' she cried wistfully. 'But people would only laugh. Look at me, in my old rags!'

'Laugh? I should think they would!' cried the two sisters. 'A fine sight *you* would be at the king's ball!'

On the great day Cinderella worked harder than ever in her life before, trying her hardest to send her sisters off to the ball looking their very best. And when the last bow was tied and the last ringlet curled, they *did* look their very best – though even that was not saying very much.

Off they went with a proud flurry of rustling skirts, out to the waiting coach, with not so much as a wave of the hand to Cinderella, let alone a thank-you. When the sound of the carriage wheels had died away and she was alone at last in the great, empty house, Cinderella crept back to her usual place by the hearth, and began to cry.

After a while she heard a knocking at the door, and drying

her eyes, went to answer. In stepped a little old woman who looked like a beggar in her tattered cloak.

'Why are you crying, child?' asked she.

'Because . . . because . . .' Cinderella did not like to say why she was crying.

'You need not tell me,' said the old lady surprisingly. 'I know quite well why you are crying. It is because you want to go to the ball.'

Cinderella stared at her.

'I am your godmother,' explained the other then. 'Your fairy godmother. And now, child, there's work to be done. Go out into the garden and fetch a pumpkin, quick!'

Cinderella was out in the garden searching for a pumpkin before she had even time to think. When she brought it back, her godmother rapped it smartly with a long black stick – or was it a wand? – and there in a trice stood a golden carriage! It winked and glittered and shone bright as the sun itself.

'Two mice!' ordered the godmother, without a blink.

Cinderella opened the pantry door and as two mice came scampering out – poof! A wave of the magic wand and they were high-stepping horses with flowing manes and rearing heads.

'What about a coachman?' murmured the godmother. 'Run and fetch the rat-trap, will you?'

Cinderella did not wait to be asked twice. Off she ran to fetch it, and next minute there stood a stout coachman with brass buttons and large three-cornered hat.

'If you look behind the watering-can beside the well,' went on the godmother, without so much as the twitch of an eyebrow, 'you will find six lizards. We could do with them, I think.'

Sure enough, there were the six lizards exactly where she had said, and a flick of that busy wand transformed them instantly into six tall footmen with dashing liveries.

'Well!' exclaimed the fairy godmother then. 'That

carriage could take a *queen* to the ball. Do you like it?'

'Oh, it's beautiful!' cried Cinderella. 'But godmother, I still can't go to the ball!'

'And why not?'

'My dress! Look at me! Whoever saw a sight like this at a king's ball?'

'That is easy enough,' replied the old lady. 'Stand still a moment, child, and shut your eyes.'

Cinderella stood quite still, her eyes tight shut. There was a slow, cool rustling, a breath of scented air and a soft silken brushing and then 'Open!' commanded that thin, high voice.

Cinderella opened her eyes.

'Oh!' she gasped. It was all she could say. 'Oh!'

About her, billowed the most beautiful dress she had ever seen, sky blue and stitched with pearls, threaded with silver. And there, beneath the hem of her skirt, glittered a pair of shining crystal shoes.

'Glass slippers!' gasped Cinderella.

'Off you go now, child,' said her godmother briskly. 'Off to the ball and enjoy yourself!'

Cinderella gathered up her shimmering skirts and stepped into the golden coach. The footmen bowed. The coachman lifted his whip.

'Wait!' cried the godmother.

Cinderella put her head out of the carriage window.

'Home by twelve sharp! Do you hear? Not a minute later!'

'I shall be back,' promised Cinderella.

'Listen for the clock,' warned her godmother. 'Not a single moment after the last stroke of twelve. If you're even a second late – '

'What?' cried Cinderella in alarm. 'What will happen, god-mother?'

The old lady waved her arms.

'Poof! Gone! Coach to pumpkin, horses to mice, coachman to rat – poof! Gone! All of it!'

'I'll remember,' cried Cinderella. 'I promise. The last stroke of twelve! Goodbye, godmother! And thank you!'

She had a last glimpse of her godmother's shabby figure and then the coach was rolling on its way. She, Cinderella, was off to a king's ball!

When at last the golden coach reached the palace gates the news was quickly spread about that a great lady, certainly a princess, had arrived at the gates. Servants and flunkeys ran to bow and open doors and make a way for Cinderella through the crowds of staring guests. For she was so beautiful that all the people stood quite still to watch her as she passed, and even the music faded as the fiddlers laid down their bows in wonder.

The king's son himself watched her walk among the whispering guests. He went to greet her, and was in love before he had even reached her side. He led her on to the floor to dance and the fiddlers picked up their bows again and began to play.

All the evening long the two of them danced together. The prince could not bear to leave Cinderella's side for even a moment. The other guests were filled with envy and curiosity, and the two ugly sisters were the angriest of all. Not a single dance had either of them had with the prince all night.

'Whoever can she be?' they cried, craning to peer at her each time she whirled by. Not for a single minute did they suspect that the beautiful stranger was none other than their sister, Cinderella.

Cinderella herself was so happy that she forgot all about the time. The great ballroom clock was already beginning to chime the hour for midnight when she suddenly remembered her godmother's warning and her own promise to be home by twelve.

'O!' she cried. 'I'm late! The time!'

Before the astonished prince could collect his wits she had darted off and was out of the ballroom and running down the great marble staircase to her waiting coach.

Six . . . seven . . . eight . . . the bell was chiming.

The coach clattered away out of the palace courtyard. At the top of the staircase the prince stood looking left and right for a sign of his vanished partner. He set the servants to search and they ran all through the palace, but in vain. She had gone. Only there, lying half way down the stairs, was a tiny glass slipper – Cinderella's. Sadly the prince picked it up and wandered away. He did not dance again that night.

Meanwhile, Cinderella was hardly out of the palace gates when – poof! The spell was broken. All in a moment she found herself out on the empty road and of the shining coach, the footman and the coachman, there was not a trace. From the corner of her eye she saw running over the road a thin dark shape, that might have been a lizard. And that was all. Clutching her thin rags about her she set off home. Safely there, she climbed up to her cold attic and fell asleep, dreaming of the ball and the handsome prince.

The prince himself did not sleep at all that night. He paced up and down his room, clasping the glass slipper.

'I must find her,' he said out loud. 'And when I have found her, I shall marry her, and make her my princess.'

Next day the king called his royal herald.

'Take this glass slipper,' he commanded, 'and search the length and breadth of my kingdom to find the young lady whose foot it fits. When you have found her, bring her to me. For she is the one the prince will marry.'

Soon the news was spread about the town and the king's herald was going from door to door reading his proclamation and trying the slipper on one foot after another. He had not known there were so many feet in the world. Then at last he came to the house where the two ugly sisters had been eagerly awaiting his visit, their hair tightly curled and their legs trembling with excitement. One of them, for sure, would fit her foot into the glass slipper and become the prince's bride.

At last they heard a loud knocking on the door, and the notes of the herald's trumpet.

'Quick!' hissed their mother. 'Sit down and look as if you weren't expecting him. And make sure one of you gets that slipper on!'

With that, she sent a servant to open the door, and next minute they were all curtseying to the king's messenger.

The two ugly sisters tried with all their might and main to fit their great feet into that dainty slipper. They squeezed and tugged and twisted and muttered and groaned, but all in vain. At last, sulky and red-faced, they gave up the attempt, trying hard not to catch their mother's eye.

'Is there no other young lady in the house?' asked the herald then. 'I have orders to miss not a single one, whoever she is.'

'No!' cried the three ladies together. 'There's no one else!'

But just then, Cinderella herself came into the room, carrying a pail. The ugly sisters tried to shoo her from the room, but the herald bowed politely to her and offered her a seat while she tried the slipper.

Cinderella sat down, held out her foot, – and slid it smoothly into the tiny glass slipper!

'It fits!' cried the ugly sisters together. 'It can't! It's a trick!'

Cinderella smiled, and taking from her pocket the other

slipper, placed it on her other foot. And at that moment, her fairy godmother appeared and with a touch of her magic wand transformed Cinderella's rags into a snow-white bridal gown.

Only then did the others recognise her as the beautiful stranger at the ball. The ugly sisters and their unkind mother hurried off, afraid of what might happen to them when their wickedness was discovered.

But Cinderella forgave them willingly, and was driven off in the king's own coach to meet her prince again. And they were married that very same day, and lived happily ever after.

The Sleeping Beauty

THERE once lived a king and queen who were married for many years without having any children. Then at last a daughter was born to them, and so delighted were they that they gave a great feast for the baby's christening. Invitations were sent to all the lords and ladies in the land and to far off kings and queens.

Thirteen fairies lived in this kingdom, but the king had only twelve golden plates to set before them, and so he had to leave one of the fairies out.

On the day of the christening the king and his guests feasted merrily, and in the evening before they left, all the fairies presented the Princess with a magic gift. One gave her the gift of wisdom, another the gift of beauty, a third wished her all the riches she desired. And so it went on until the eleventh fairy had spoken, when suddenly the glittering crowd of guests parted and between them went the thirteenth fairy, all in black. She looked neither left nor right and greeted no one. She stopped by the side of the baby's cradle and lifted her arms like great black wings and cried in a terrible voice,

'When the Princess is fifteen years old, she shall prick herself with a spindle and fall down dead!'

Her arms fell and in a great silence she turned and went out of the hall.

Now the twelfth fairy still had not made her gift. It was beyond her power to undo the wicked spell entirely, but she was able to soften it, by saying,

'When the Princess pricks herself with a spindle, she shall not die, but fall into a deep sleep lasting for a hundred years.'

Even this seemed tragedy enough to the King and Queen,

and they gave orders that all the spindles in the land should be burned. As the Princess grew up, growing wiser and lovelier and kinder each day, the fairy's curse began to seem very faint and far away, so that they hardly thought of it at all.

On the Princess's fifteenth birthday a party was held at the Palace. The Princess begged for a game of hide and seek. The guests scattered and the Princess herself began to run up and down the stone corridors, looking for a hiding place. At last she came to a crumbling tower that she had never noticed before.

'They will never find me here!' she thought.

She climbed the narrow, winding stairs and came to a studded door with a great rusty key in the lock. The Princess turned it and went inside.

There in the cold stone room sat an old woman with a spindle, spinning flax. The Princess stared. All the spindles in the kingdom had disappeared long ago, because of the fairy's curse, and so she had never set eyes on one before.

'Good day, Granny,' said the Princess. She had quite forgotten the game of hide-and-seek. 'What are you doing?'

'I am spinning,' replied the old woman, nodding her head.

'And what is this that whirls round so merrily?' asked the Princess. With these words she took the spindle and tried to spin too.

But she had scarcely touched it before the curse was fulfilled and she pricked her finger with the spindle. She fell back on to the bed nearby, and the old woman, her work done, went away down the stone stairs with her evil laughter echoing about her.

At the very moment when the Princess fell to the bed her guests, too, closed their eyes and slept just where they happened

to be – some in cupboards, some behind pillars and others under the great four poster beds. Even the King and Queen fell asleep in the great hall. Their courtiers yawned and rubbed their eyes and soon were sprawling on the strewn rushes. The horses lay sleeping in the stables, the dogs in the yard, the doves on the roof, the flies on the wall. Even the fire on the hearth stopped its flickering and the meat on the spit stopped crackling. The cook, who was about to box the scullion's ears, began to snore with her arm still raised for the blow. Outside, the wind dropped. Not a bough stirred, not a twig, not a leaf. All slept.

Round the castle a hedge of briers began to grow up, minute by minute. It grew higher and higher, surrounding the whole castle with live green walls of thorn and bramble. Soon nothing could be seen from the outside world, not even a turret, not even a flag on the roof. Within, the clocks ticked to a standstill, the dust settled, there was nothing but sleep and silence.

A legend grew up as years went by about the sleeping Brier Rose, as the Princess was called. Princes came from far off lands to try to force their way through the high thickets. But the greedy thorns clutched them like hands so that they could never escape and were left there to die.

Then, one day, when the hundred years were nearly up, a bold and handsome prince rode by. He met an old man working in the woods, who told him the legend of the beautiful sleeping Princess. He begged the Prince not to try to enter, and warned him of the terrible fate that had befallen the rest.

'I am not afraid,' replied the Prince. 'I am determined to go and see Brier Rose with my own eyes.'

He rode to the thicket, never knowing that this very day the one hundred years were ended, and the Princess would wake from her spellbound sleep. As the Prince drew near, he saw to his astonishment that the hedge was covered with large and beautiful flowers. They seemed to be unfurling their

petals even as he watched. As he rode up the briers curled back
and made way for him so that he could pass unharmed, and
then closed up again into a hedge behind him.

In the courtyard he found brindled dogs lying asleep, nose
on paws. He saw doves on the roof, heads under their wings.
He pushed the door and entered the silent palace and saw
there the King and Queen themselves, lying by the throne.
The Prince had to step over the sleeping forms of guards and
courtiers and passed next through the kitchen where the cook
had stood for a hundred years with her arm raised ready to
box the scullion's ears. Nearby sat a maid who had been fixed

in time while she plucked the black feathers from a fowl on her knee.

The Prince went tiptoe through all the palace, and so great was the hush that he could hear his own breathing. Then at last he came to the ancient tower and climbing the winding stair came to the chamber where Brier Rose lay sleeping.

The Princess looked so beautiful lying there that the Prince knelt by the bedside and kissed her gently on the lips. And to his wonder, Brier Rose opened her eyes and gazed up at him. Then she sat up and yawned. And then she stretched and asked the time of day for all the world as if she had woken from a nap.

The Prince and Brier Rose went down together and found the whole palace astir. The hounds sprang up and wagged their tails, the doves on the roof stretched their wings and fluttered off to the fields. The flies buzzed, the fire leapt, the meat began to roast. And the scullion received at last the box on the ears that had threatened him for a hundred years, and let out a yell that woke the maid who was plucking the fowl.

Everything went on as if nothing had ever happened, as if a century were no more than the twinkling of an eye. And soon the dust of a hundred years was flying in clouds through open doors and windows as the palace was prepared for the wedding of Brier Rose and her gallant prince.

The Princess and the Pea

THERE was once a Prince who wished to marry a Princess, but she must be a *real* Princess. He travelled the world far and wide in search of her, but though he met many Princesses of every kind, he could never be quite certain in his own heart whether or not she was a *real* Princess. There was always some little fault with each one that seemed to show him that she was not his true bride.

At last, sad at heart, because he really *did* wish to marry, he returned home.

One night soon afterwards there was a terrible storm. The thunder roared and the lightning flashed and the rain came down in sheets and in the midst of it all came a knocking at the palace gates.

The King went to see who was there, and there stood a Princess, looking a very sad sight indeed. Water trickled from her hair and poured from her clothes and her shoes squelched as she stepped inside. But she said that she was a real Princess and that she wished to stay for the night.

'We shall see whether she is a real Princess or not,' thought the old Queen, who found it hard to believe that the girl was a Princess at all, with her bedraggled locks and ruined clothes.

She went into the guest chamber and there made up the bed in a special way. First she took all the bedclothes off and laid a single pea on the bedstead. Then she took twenty mattresses and piled them on top of the pea, and next piled twenty feather beds on top of the mattresses. The Princess was shown to her chamber and climbed up into the bed.

Next morning when she rose the Queen asked her,
'And did you sleep well last night?'

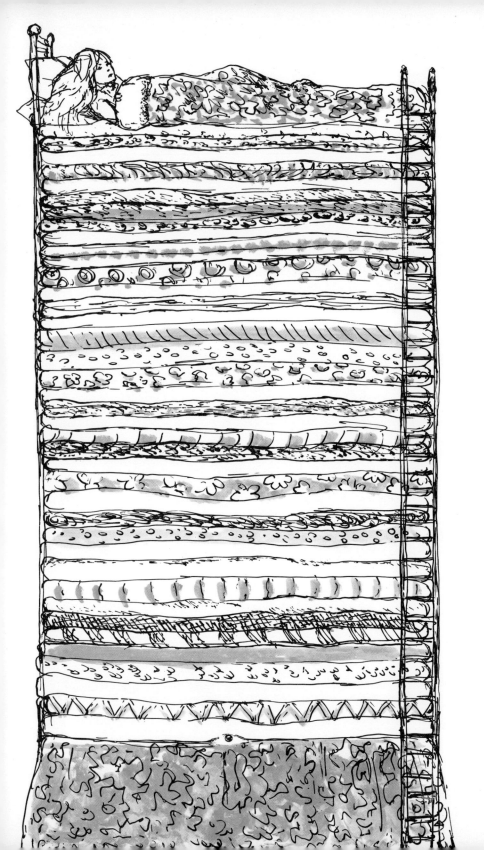

'I hardly had a wink!' replied the Princess. 'I tossed and turned the whole night through. I could feel something hard digging into me, and sure enough, I'm black and blue all over this morning. It was terrible!'

At this, they all saw at once that here, at last, was a real Princess. After all, she had felt a single pea through twenty mattresses and twenty feather beds. Nobody but a real Princess could have so delicate a sense of feeling.

And so the Prince took her gladly as his wife, certain that at last he had found a real Princess. And as for the pea, it was taken and put into a museum, where it may still be seen, if no one has stolen it.

And this, you may depend upon it, is a true story.

Puss in Boots

ONCE upon a time there was a poor Miller who had three sons. When he died he had nothing to leave them but his mill, his ass and his cat. So he left the mill to his eldest son, the ass to his second son, and his youngest son had to be contented with the cat.

'Whatever shall I do?' cried he. 'It's all very well for my brothers, but once I've killed my cat and sold his skin to make gloves, I'll have nothing at all in the world!'

Master Puss heard all this.

'Sell my skin to make gloves?' he mewed. 'You can do better than this with me, dear Master. In fact, if you do everything that I tell you, there's a fortune to be made!'

The young man was very surprised and pleased to find that he had such a clever cat, and readily agreed to do as he was bid.

'First,' said Puss, 'you must find me a pair of stout leather boots, and a sack.'

The Miller's son found both and brought them to him, and Puss drew on the great boots with a loud purring and swaggered up and down to show them off. He then slung the sack over his shoulder and went into the nearby countryside.

He stopped at last in a field that was full of rabbit warrens, and laid down the sack by the largest burrow. Then Puss himself lay down by the sack with his head hanging limply to one side as if he had broken his neck.

After a time, up came a fine fat rabbit, saw the 'dead' cat, and went sniffing into the sack to find the bran and lettuce leaves that Puss had placed there.

Up jumped Puss, pulled the strings of the sack tight, and the rabbit was caught.

That evening Puss came to the door of the palace carrying
a brace of plump rabbits, and demanded to see the King. The
Chamberlain was charmed by the sight of this impudent Puss
in his fine boots, and led the way to the throne room.

Puss made a sweeping bow and laid the rabbits at the King's
feet, saying,

'Your Majesty, here is a gift from my master, My Lord the
Marquis of Carabas!'

The King was delighted both with the gift and with Puss
himself, and gave orders that the cat was to be allowed to call
whenever he pleased.

Puss purred. This suited him very well. Each day he went
poaching in the king's woods and each evening he went to
the palace with his catch and offered it to the King as 'a gift
from My Lord the Marquis of Carabas.' Besides this, the Miller's
son had as many rabbits and pheasants as he wanted, as well as
the presents that Puss brought back from the King himself.

One day Puss came back from the palace in great excitement.

'O Master, Master!' he mewed. 'The time has come for
your fortune to be made! Just do as I tell you, and all will be

well. All you have to do is to go down and bathe in the river. At noon, the King will ride by with his only child, the Princess. You must be in the water when they arrive. Don't be alarmed whatever should happen, and leave it all to me!'

By now the Miller's son was ready to do anything his cat asked, and so next day he went down to the river as he had been told. There he stripped off his worn and ragged clothes and plunged into the water. As soon as he had done so, Puss ran up, took the heap of clothes, and hid them in a ditch. Then he waited till he heard the wheels of the king's carriage and ran out on to the road crying,

'Help! Help! My Master, the Marquis of Carabas is drowning!'

When the King saw it was his favourite, the Puss in Boots who brought him so many presents, he ordered his servants to hurry to the river.

'Alas, alas!' cried the cunning Puss as he led the way. 'Wicked robbers set upon my Master and robbed him of his fine clothes and jewels and everything he had. Then they threw him into the river to drown, and I myself cannot swim. Save him, quickly, before he drowns! O my dear Master!'

The servants ran and pulled the Miller's son out of the water and one of them went running back to the palace to fetch a suit of the King's own clothes. Puss led him to the King and introduced him as 'My most noble Master, My Lord the Marquis of Carabas.' The King was so charmed by his noble appearance that he invited him into the carriage to join himself and the Princess on their ride. Puss purred.

But there was still work to be done. Puss ran on ahead, tail up in the air, till he came to a field of corn where men were haymaking.

'Good people!' cried Puss, his whiskers curling, 'Soon the King is coming this way. He is sure to stop and ask who this fine field belongs to. And if you do not say that it belongs to My Lord the Marquis of Carabas, I will have you all chopped up as small as mincemeat!'

Off he bounded, and when the king stopped to admire the hay

and ask to whom it belonged, all the man in the field replied,

'It belongs to My Lord the Marquis of Carabas!'

'What fine hay you have, Marquis,' said the King, and the Miller's son bowed politely.

By this time, Puss himself had reached a great cornfield where men were cutting the ripe corn with sickles and binding it into sheaves. Puss called out to them, and they were so amazed to see a Puss in boots that they too obeyed his orders, and when the King stopped to ask to whom the corn belonged, meekly replied,

'It belongs to My Lord the Marquis of Carabas!'

Meanwhile, Puss had come to the castle where lived the wicked Ogre who was the real owner of all the land about. He was so cruel that anyone who disobeyed him was straightway killed and served up for the Ogre's dinner. No one could fight him, because he had the power of turning himself into any animal he chose – and no one could fight single-handed against a savage tiger or raging wolf.

Puss came striding up to the castle gates, bared his teeth at the guards and went straight into the hall where the Ogre sat.

'What's this?' growled the Ogre, chewing at a bone. 'Who are you, and how dare you enter my castle?'

'O Your Eminence, O Your Excellency, O Your *Most* Excellency,' mewed Puss, bowing so low that his ears brushed the ground, 'I am a traveller, out to see the wonders of the world. And of all the wonders of the world, I have heard that you are the wonderfullest. Ever since I was a kitten I have heard tales of you that I could scarcely believe. They say you can change yourself into any animal you choose. Is it true? I can hardly believe it!'

'Believe it!' cried the Ogre, crunching his bone, 'Believe it! I'll show you!'

Next minute, there stood a great yellow lion lashing its tail and roaring, and Puss himself was up in the rafters, arching his back and spitting.

The Ogre changed back into his own shape again, bellowing
with laughter, and Puss came carefully down from the roof.

'O sir, O noble and mighty Sir,' cried Puss, 'Forgive me
for not believing! Now I have seen it with my own eyes, I
see how truly wonderful you are. But there is one *tiny* thing
that worries me.'

'What?' roared the ogre, tearing the leg from a roast ox.
'What, miserable little cat?'

'Please, sir, noble sir,' said Puss, 'You are so noble and fine
that to be able to change yourself into a lion, the king of the
beasts himself, is almost to be expected. But how could so
great and powerful a person as yourself change himself into

some very small and humble creature, such as a mouse, for instance? That, I'm sure, is quite impossible!'

'Impossible?' yelled the Ogre, snapping the ox bone in half. 'Wretched little creature, I'll show you!'

A moment later the Ogre was gone and a small brown mouse scampered over the floor. Puss poised, ears back, tail a-twitch, pounced – and gobbled the mouse in a trice. And that was the end of the Ogre. Puss purred.

All the Ogre's servants came running into the hall, laughing and crying for joy. Puss jumped up on to a table and held up a paw for silence.

'I have killed your cruel master,' he said, 'and now a new master is coming who will treat you wisely and well. But if you do not do as I tell you, I will have you all chopped as small as mincemeat!'

This the people could readily believe.

'All you have to do,' said Puss, 'is to tell the King when he enquires, that this castle and all its lands belong to My Lord the Marquis of Carabas!'

And so, when evening came and the King's coach came rolling out of the sunset and over the drawbridge, hundreds of servants in rich liveries stood in lines on either side. Puss came forward and opened the carriage door with a sweeping bow.'

'Welcome, Your Majesty!' he mewed. 'Welcome to the castle of My Lord the Marquis of Carabas!'

'This too?' cried the King, astonished, looking about him at the magnificent castle and throngs of servants. 'Truly, sir, you are worthy to be a member of the royal family!'

Puss hid a smile behind his paw and led the way indoors where a splendid banquet was prepared. At the end of it the King, who had noticed that the Princess and the young man

were holding hands under the table, wiped his mouth on a
napkin, hiccoughed happily, and said,

'Marquis, I know of no one whom I would rather have
for a son-in-law than yourself. I can see that my daughter
likes you, and if she is willing, let the wedding take place
immediately.'

The Miller's youngest son held his breath. Was he really to
become a Prince – perhaps a King?

Then 'I will marry him gladly,' replied the king's daughter.

Puss purred.

Aladdin and the Wonderful Lamp

ONCE, long ago, in a city of China, there lived a poor tailor called Mustapha, with his wife and only son, Aladdin. Both the father and mother were so hard worked that they had very little time to spare for Aladdin, and so he grew up very wild and mischievous. By the time he was fifteen he still had not learned a trade so that he could help his parents, and he would spend all day long idling in the streets with his friends.

Even when his father died the poor widow was forced to spin cotton from morning till night to keep herself and her son. Aladdin still spent his time loafing in the streets.

One day a tall, dark stranger with rich flowing robes came up to him and said,

'Surely you are Aladdin, the son of my long-lost brother?'

'My father has been dead a long time,' replied Aladdin, astonished to find that he had such a rich relation.

The stranger was really a Magician from Africa, and no relation to Aladdin at all, but he pretended to be very sorry to hear that his so-called brother was dead. He took Aladdin to a nearby shop and bought him sweetmeats, then pressed a purse full of gold into Aladdin's hand and said,

'Take this to your poor widowed mother. And tell her that tomorrow her dead husband's brother will come and talk to her.'

Next day the Magician did visit the widow, and although she had never heard her husband mention that he had a brother, the sight of such finery and riches quite overwhelmed her, and soon Aladdin was calling the Magican Uncle.

A few days afterwards the Magician took Aladdin for a walk outside the city towards the mountains. As he went along he talked about the strange and distant lands he had visited, about Africa, and about the great fortune that was surely in store for Aladdin himself if he only did as his new-found Uncle told him. Aladdin's head was soon turned by all this, and he eagerly said that he was ready to do all that the Magician commanded.

At the foot of the mountain the Magician stopped, cleared away the dead leaves with his cane, and drew a circle in the dust. He closed his eyes, muttered a charm under his breath, and uncovered a stone trapdoor in the earth itself. Aladdin watched in amazement.

Then the Magician drew from his finger a ring, a green stone set in silver, and placed it on the first finger of Aladdin's own right hand.

'This magic ring will keep you safe wherever you go,' he said. 'And now listen what you must do.'

Aladdin listened.

'First,' said the Uncle, 'you must lift the stone trap door and go right down under the earth. There you will find beautiful gardens, and you must walk through them till you come to a rocky shelf where there stands a lighted lamp. Blow out the flame, pour away the oil, and bring it back to me here.'

Aladdin obediently lifted the trapdoor and went down the first few steps. He turned and looked back into his Uncle's dark, greedy face.

'All the treasures of the world will be yours if you do as I say,' said the Magician.

So Aladdin took a last look at the sky and the light of day, and began his journey under the earth. As the Magician had told him, he passed through beautiful gardens filled with fruits and flowers that glittered and sparkled. But these parks were strangely silent, for not a bird sang nor a living creature stirred. All was glittering and still.

Aladdin hastened on till he came to the rocky ledge and

found the lamp, just as he had been promised. He pushed it
into the front of his robe and on the way back stopped to
gather the marvellous fruits of the garden, stuffing them, too,
into his robe and filling his pockets and his purse. When he
reached the stone steps his uncle's face appeared at the top,
blocking the sky.

'Pass up the lamp, dear Nephew,' he cried. 'And my silver
ring. Then I will give you a hand to climb out.'

But the lamp was buried beneath the stolen fruits, and
Aladdin called back,

'Help me up, first, Uncle, then I will give you the lamp
and the ring!'

The Magician's face grew stormy.

'The ring and the lamp!' he cried. 'Give them to me, boy!'

'No,' replied Aladdin. 'Not until I am safely out!'

'The lamp!' screamed the Magician in a fury. 'The ring!'

Aladdin, seeing his rage, was more determined than ever
not to part with either until he was safely out of the cave.
There he stood, stubbornly shaking his head, while his Uncle
stamped and raged above him. At last, with a final shriek,

the Magician slammed down the stone trapdoor and was gone.

The sky disappeared in an instant. It was so quiet that Aladdin could hear his own breathing. He reached up and battered at the trapdoor with his fists, crying,

'Let me out! Let me out!'

All in vain. Silence. Darkness. Slowly Aladdin turned and wandered back into the gardens. He was hungry now, and looked longingly at the glowing fruits, but knew that they were made of stones, of priceless rubies and emeralds and diamonds. At that moment Aladdin would have exchanged every single one of them for a ripe green fig or a bunch of plump grapes.

At last Aladdin, ravenously hungry and in despair, sat down and began to weep. He lifted his hand to brush away the tears, and in doing so, rubbed the Magician's green stone ring against his cheek. Next minute a great and awful Genie, towering like a flame, came shooting out of the ground before him.

'What is the will of my lord, the Master of the Ring?' said the Genie, bowing low. 'I am the Slave of the Ring. Speak! To hear is to obey!'

'Then take me out of this horrible place!' sobbed Aladdin. 'Take me home!'

Next minute Aladdin was on his own street at his own door, and rushed inside to embrace his mother and tell her all that had happened.

The following day, Aladdin woke up hungry, and asked his mother to take the old lamp he had brought back from the cave, down to the market.

'We shan't get much for it,' he said, 'but enough to buy some food.'

'I will give it a clean first,' replied his mother. 'Then perhaps it will fetch more money.'

She took a rag, and had no sooner begun to rub the lamp when a giant Genie rushed out of it and stood towering

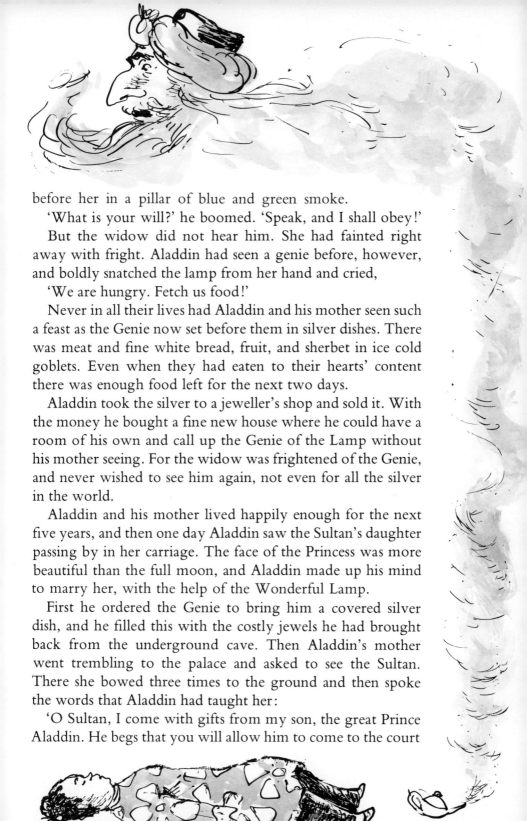

before her in a pillar of blue and green smoke.

'What is your will?' he boomed. 'Speak, and I shall obey!'

But the widow did not hear him. She had fainted right away with fright. Aladdin had seen a genie before, however, and boldly snatched the lamp from her hand and cried,

'We are hungry. Fetch us food!'

Never in all their lives had Aladdin and his mother seen such a feast as the Genie now set before them in silver dishes. There was meat and fine white bread, fruit, and sherbet in ice cold goblets. Even when they had eaten to their hearts' content there was enough food left for the next two days.

Aladdin took the silver to a jeweller's shop and sold it. With the money he bought a fine new house where he could have a room of his own and call up the Genie of the Lamp without his mother seeing. For the widow was frightened of the Genie, and never wished to see him again, not even for all the silver in the world.

Aladdin and his mother lived happily enough for the next five years, and then one day Aladdin saw the Sultan's daughter passing by in her carriage. The face of the Princess was more beautiful than the full moon, and Aladdin made up his mind to marry her, with the help of the Wonderful Lamp.

First he ordered the Genie to bring him a covered silver dish, and he filled this with the costly jewels he had brought back from the underground cave. Then Aladdin's mother went trembling to the palace and asked to see the Sultan. There she bowed three times to the ground and then spoke the words that Aladdin had taught her:

'O Sultan, I come with gifts from my son, the great Prince Aladdin. He begs that you will allow him to come to the court to ask for the hand of your daughter, the beautiful Princess.'

The Sultan was not much impressed by the widow, but when the lid of the silver dish was lifted and he saw the heap of jewels, he thought to himself,

'This Aladdin must be richer even than myself! Certainly I must take a look at him!'

Next day Aladdin dressed in his finest clothes and rode to the palace on a snow white horse. As he went through the streets he and his servants scattered gold and silver pieces among the crowds who flocked to see them, and the people all scurried to pick them up, crying,

'Long live Prince Aladdin! May he live forever!'

The Sultan himself agreed that Aladdin should marry the Princess if he could build a palace as fine as that of the Sultan himself. The Genie of the Lamp and his helpers built the palace so swiftly that one day there was nothing there, and the next there was a pure white palace with roofs of sparkling gold, sprung up like a mushroom overnight. Aladdin and the Princess were married that very week, and at the wedding Aladdin again scattered gifts of gold and silver among the crowds. The people cheered and clapped, and the Sultan told himself what a fine new son-in-law he had.

Five years passed. Then, far away in Africa, the wicked Magician chanced to look one day in his magic glass, and saw pictures there of Aladdin living splendidly in his palace with his Princess.

'What?' he cried. 'Aladdin? Alive and well? I thought him dead ten years ago, under the mountain. He lives in a palace, does he, with a Princess for wife? Only the Wonderful Lamp could have done this!'

He set off straightaway for China, determined that this time Aladdin should not outwit him, and that he would have the Wonderful Lamp for himself. When he reached Aladdin's city, he bought a cart and filled it with bright new copper lamps. Then he went through the streets, crying,

'New lamps for old! New lamps for old!'

All the delighted housewives ran out to him with their old lamps and exchanged them for the shiny new ones. On the seventh day, the Magician chanced at last to pass under the window where the Princess was sitting alone.

'What a bargain!' she cried, when she heard the Magician's call. 'I know my Lord Aladdin has a dirty old lamp in his room, and how he will praise me when he discovers that I have exchanged it for a brand new one!'

She gave Aladdin's key to her handmaiden and sent her running to fetch the lamp.

No sooner did the Magician have the Wonderful Lamp in his hands, when he ran with it into the hall of Aladdin's palace and summoned up the Genie, smouldering in his blue flame. In a flash the palace with everyone in it was spirited away to a lonely desert in the middle of Africa. There the Magician told the Princess that Aladdin had been slain by robbers, and begged her to marry him. But she would not listen, and sat weeping with terror and grief.

When the Sultan found that the palace had vanished with his daughter in it, he ordered Aladdin to be thrown into prison, and refused even to listen to him. But all the people of the city to whom Aladdin had given so many presents of gold and silver, came to the palace in a great crowd and set Aladdin free.

Fearlessly Aladdin went and stood before the angry Sultan.

'Have no fear,' he said. 'Before the moon has risen again you shall find the palace in its rightful place, and your daughter safe and sound within.'

He then went alone into a nearby grove and rubbed his green and silver ring. Straightway the Genie rose before him, and at Aladdin's command took him to Africa and set him down by the Princess's side.

When they had embraced, the Princess told Aladdin that the Magician always kept the Wonderful Lamp hidden in his robes, and that he would be returning to the palace before nightfall. Aladdin called up the Genie of the Ring, and the Genie said,

'To hear is to obey, O Lord. But against the Genie of the Lamp I have no power, unless you yourself are greater than he who holds the Lamp!'

Aladdin hid himself, and waited for the Magician to return, knowing that this was a battle he must fight for himself. As soon as he heard the Magician's voice, Aladdin stepped out, and cried,

'Your hour has come, O wicked one! May all your crimes be visited on your head!'

The Magician, forgetting the Wonderful Lamp, flew into a blind fury at Aladdin's words, and struck him in the face. And in that very instant he fell down dead at Aladdin's feet, while outside a great storm of thunder and lightning shook the palace.

Aladdin took the Wonderful Lamp and rubbed it, and next minute the Palace was back in China, in its rightful place, there to stay for ever more. And the old Sultan, looking out of his window next morning, rubbed his eyes and blinked when he saw the sun shining on its golden turrets. He hurried round and begged Aladdin's forgiveness, which he willingly gave. And Aladdin and his Princess lived in peace and happiness for the rest of their lives, thanks to the Genie of the Wonderful Lamp.

Dick Whittington and His Cat

ONCE upon a time, long long ago, a little orphan boy named Dick Whittington came from the country up to the great city of London.

'The streets of London are paved with gold,' he had heard the villagers say as they told tales under the chestnuts on summer evenings, or by the fireside in winter. And so Dick set out to see for himself. He was ten years old, alone in the world, and determined to make his fortune.

He was hungry and footsore when he came to London after days of travelling through the countryside, begging food and sleeping in barns and under hedges. But when he saw the domes and spires ahead of him against the sky, he hurried his pace, eager for a glimpse of those marvellous golden streets.

But as he entered the city at last, the stones beneath his feet were grey – as grey as ever they had been in any other town he had known. On and on he walked, hoping with every mile that he would round a sudden corner and see before him a street of purest gold, where he could stoop and gather up the golden cobbles and cram his pockets with them and be rich for the rest of his life.

But the people of London did not *look* rich – they did not

even look so well and happy as the villagers at home. They walked in tatters with bent shoulders, though now and then a rich coach would go rolling by, with liveried footmen hanging on behind. Dick slept that night huddled in a doorway, and next morning, wandering through the narrow streets in a thin drizzle of rain, he suddenly lost heart, and said to himself,

'I have come on a wild goose chase. I shall go back home, to my own village, and work in the fields and be as happy as I can.'

Sad at heart, he began to retrace his footsteps, and soon was outside the city and walking in the open country back towards home. He sat down propped against a milestone, and opened his bundle to find his last piece of cheese. As he sat there, the sound of bells was wafted over the fields from the city churches. They rang sweet and clear, and as Dick listened, he seemed to hear what they were saying:

Turn again Whitting-ton
Thou worthy cit-izen
Lord Mayor of Lon-don!

He leapt to his feet and stood with ears cocked. Again the peals came on a light wind, and as Dick stared back towards the city the sun suddenly struck through the clouds and shone on the wet roofs, turning them to gold.

Turn again Whitting-ton
Thou worthy cit-izen
Lord Mayor of Lon-don!

'And so I will!' cried Dick. And he picked up his knapsack and turned his face again towards the city.

That night he slept on a doorstep again, but this time he was discovered at dawn by a red-faced Cook, who opened the door and stirred him with her foot.

'You'll make a fine scullion!' cried she. 'Lazy layabout – asleep at this hour! Five o'clock in the morning, and still fast asleep! You'd best come in and have breakfast and get started working!'

Dick followed her inside, scarcely believing his luck. He had not known that the household was looking for a scullion, but now, it seemed, he had the job, and was glad of it. He was given a room up in the garret, paid a penny a week and given a new suit of clothes. He worked from morning till night in the kitchen, and Cook scolded him if he did not wash behind his ears and keep his nails clean. But if he did, she would cut him a big slice of jam pie, so Dick's face was usually red and shining with soap and water.

This house belonged to a rich merchant named Fitzwarren, who had a little girl of nine years old called Alice. One day, she came down to the kitchen wearing a blue silk dress and a coral necklace. She stared at Dick, who was shelling peas in a corner.

'Are you the raggedy boy who came from the country?' she asked. 'You look quite clean to me.'

'That's because Cook chases me with her broom if I'm dirty,' replied Dick. 'Besides, I'm used to being clean now, and quite like it.'

Alice drew up a stool nearby and asked Dick questions about his old life in the country and how he had come to London. So Dick told her about how he had set back home when he had found that the streets of London were not paved with gold after all, and how he had heard the bells calling him back:

Turn again Whitting-ton
Thou worthy cit-izen
Lord Mayor of Lon-don!

'And perhaps I *shall* be Lord Mayor, one day,' he said, because even if he did sleep in a garret and spend the day scouring dishes and sweeping floors, he still had his dreams.

Alice laughed and spread out her silken skirts and said,

'Well, you are quite a clean boy now, and sometimes I may come down to the kitchen and talk to you. But you are only a scullion and I am a lady, so you may not smile at me unless I smile at you first.'

After that, Alice used to come down and talk to Dick sometimes, and he was well pleased with his life, except for one thing. The garret where he slept was overrun by rats, that scampered all over his bed when he was asleep. So he saved his wages and spent threepence on the biggest cat he could find. Soon all the rats had disappeared, and the cat would purr on Dick's bed at night instead, and keep his feet warm.

In those days, when merchants sent a ship to trade with Africa, everyone who worked for them could send in the ship a bale of goods, whatever he liked. This was called a 'Venture' or 'Adventure'. One day, Fitzwarren said to Dick,

'Next week my new ship sails for Africa. What will you send as a Venture?'

'I have nothing,' replied Dick. 'Nothing but my cat, that is.'

'Then you had better send the cat,' said the merchant. 'Every single one of us must send a Venture, or it will mean bad luck for the new ship.'

So when the ship sailed, Dick's cat went with it, and it came to port in Africa, where the rich Sultan was eager to see all the fine things from London. The Captain spread out the cargo before the Sultan and his five hundred and fifty-five wives. They were delighted. The Captain of the ship had more African gold to take back to London than ever before.

'Now there is only the cat left,' he said to himself. 'And for that, I will receive more than its weight in gold!'

While he had been trading with the Sultan, rats and mice had been scurrying about them the whole time, nibbling at sacks, running up curtains, and even biting the Sultan's queens. When the Captain went to make his farewells, he went with the cat perched on his shoulder.

In the palace, the mice and rats were squealing and running about as usual. The cat sprang from the Captain's shoulder and in less than five minutes had killed fifty of them and sent the rest to their holes. Then she went and sat at the Sultan's feet, purring, and he ordered a silver dish of thick yellow cream to be set before her.

The Sultan had never seen a cat before, and knew at once that he must have this wonderful creature for his own.

'I shall give you five hundred pieces of gold for the cat,' said he, plucking at his turban.

'O Mighty Sultan, may you live forever,' replied the Captain. 'But if we give up this wonderful cat, the ship will be overrun by rats on our return voyage. They will eat up all the food, and we may starve to death.'

'That, indeed, would be a thousand pities,' replied the Sultan. 'I see that I must give more for the cat to make the risk worth

your while. What do you say to a thousand gold pieces and this diamond from my own turban?'

The Captain stared at the diamond, and swallowed. It was as large as a quail's egg and flashing blue fire.

'We will take the risk, O Mighty Sultan,' he replied. 'The cat is yours.'

When the ship came into London docks, all Fitzwarren's men were there to receive the money paid on their Ventures. When it came to Dick's turn, he asked if he could have his cat again, never believing that it had fetched a single gold piece, let alone a fortune. When the Captain told him the tale, Dick could hardly believe him till the Captain showed him the sack of gold and the enormous diamond.

The merchant slapped Dick on the back and called him 'Son Richard'.

'You shall have a share in my next new ship,' said he. 'Lord Mayor of London, eh? Those bells of yours could have spoken truth, it seems!'

Alice had told her father the story of what the bells had said, and he had thought it a good jest. Now, he began to wonder. If this boy could make a fortune out of a single cat, what else might he not do?

Out of his money Dick bought Alice a velvet sash and Cook a silken dress and a silver pin. The rest he ventured in Fitzwarren's next ship, and when the ship returned, Dick was twice as rich. When the ship after that came home, Dick was twice as rich again. By now he was a fine and handsome young man.

'Cook's boy,' said Mistress Alice, 'you may smile at me now, for I have smiled at you first.'

Dick smiled at her. One thing led to another, and soon they were married. The Lord Mayor himself came to the wedding, wearing his red robes and driving in a gilt coach with ten white horses.

'There!' whispered Alice. 'See how fine you'll look, Dick, when *you're* Lord Mayor!'

And ten years later, Dick *was* Lord Mayor. He went before the King and knelt before him, and the King laid a sword on Dick's shoulder.

'Rise up, Sir Richard!' said he.

So Dick was Sir Richard Whittington, Lord Mayor of London, as the bells had promised him so many years ago as he had leaned on the milestone in the drizzling rain. And sometimes Sir Richard Whittington would still go out of London on a Sunday to that very place, and think about the cat who had made his fortune, and listen again to what the bells were saying:

Turn again Whittington,
Thou worthy citizen,
Lord Mayor of London!

The Fir Tree

THERE was once a little fir tree that grew in a wood. It had a warm, sunny spot and was surrounded by other fir trees and pines, some of them so high that their branches seemed to touch the very sky. The fir tree would gaze and gaze up at their great spreading branches and long to grow big and tall itself and to scratch its own needles against the sky.

The tree was so lost in staring up at the sky that it hardly even noticed all the things that were going on about it on the ground. The village children came out to pick wild raspberries and picnicked by the little tree. There they would sit and eat the fruit out of their jugs, and often one of them would say,

'What a pretty little fir tree!'

But this did not please the fir tree at all. It wanted to be big. It wanted the birds to come and nest in its branches, and longed to be high up where the great winds blew by, so that it could sway grandly and nod its head as the others did.

The sun that shone down through the boughs of the forest whispered gently,

'Do not be in such a hurry, little fir tree. You must wait, wait! I will help you to grow – feel how warm I am! But you must wait, wait . . .'

In the winter, when the ground was white and glistening all around, a little hare would come crunching over the snow and leap over the top of the little tree. How the tree hated it, and drew up its branches in annoyance! But two winters went by, and by the third winter the tree had grown so high that the hare had to go round it. Then the tree waved its boughs with pleasure and held them out to catch the falling snow.

Every autumn the woodmen came and the sound of snapping boughs and crashing trees echoed through the forest. Only the tallest and straightest trees were felled, and then their boughs were lopped and they were carried away, lashed on carts.

'Where do they go?' said the fir tree longingly to the swallows and the stork who came in the spring.

The stork replied, 'When I fly over the ocean from Egypt, I meet fine ships with tall masts. And when I circle the mast, I think I smell fir!'

'Ah!' cried the little tree. 'They go to sea, they discover the whole world!' And he stretched and stretched, reaching for the sky.

'Wait, wait!' whispered the sunbeams. And the wind kissed the tree and the dew shed tears on it, but the fir tree didn't understand.

At Christmas, the woodmen's axes rang out again in the forest, and the village children came running out to watch the work.

'Why do they fell only the small trees?' wondered the little fir tree. 'Why – look at that one! It's hardly bigger than me – and that one is even smaller! Perhaps this is a chance for me!'

'We know where they go! We know where they go!' twittered the sparrows. 'We've been to the town and looked in through the windows. And we've seen them set in the

middle of the warm room and decorated as if they were kings, hung with stars and golden apples and gingerbread and toys. And at night they are lit with hundreds and hundreds of candles and all the people gather round them – it's the most marvellous sight you have ever seen!'

The fir tree made the sparrows repeat their story again and again, and all through the next year dreamed of it and longed for Christmas time to come. It hardly noticed the spring and the flowers, the summer with its hot sun and singing insects, or the autumn when the sun's rays stretched longer to reach down and touch the tree's boughs.

'O fir tree,' whispered the sun, before it left for the last time, 'Wait, wait! Be glad you are young and strong, and enjoy your life while you can!'

But now it was nearly Christmas, and the little fir tree was tall and straight with thick, dark green branches, and it knew that its dreams were at last to come true. And sure enough, when the woodmen came, they picked it out and cut it down first of all. And as the axe went through its stem the little fir tree was so overcome with joy that it hardly even noticed the pain, or the dizzy fall to the ground, or the long uncomfortable ride to town on a wagon.

All the trees were unloaded in a yard, and a man came and picked out the fir tree and said, 'Here, we'll have this one.'

Two servants came and took the tree inside into a big warm room with a fire burning in the grate. There were richly coloured carpets and chairs and sofas of shining silk. There the tree was stood up in a big barrel filled with sand, and it gazed proudly about, waiting to be crowned like a king, and seeing its friends the sparrows twittering on the window sill outside.

Everything happened as the sparrows had promised. The tree's boughs were decked with glittering stars and golden apples. It received little bags of sweets wrapped in coloured paper, toys and dolls. Then more than a hundred candles,

green, red, blue and white were fixed to its branches, and
last of all a great star of gold tinsel was set right at the very top.

'I am crowned at last!' breathed the little fir tree, and stood
tiptoe, breath held, in case a branch should move and the
treasure fall to the ground.

'Tonight we will light the candles,' said the servants. Then
they went out and left the tree alone in the dancing firelight
to hug its glory and admire its reflection in the window panes.

When it grew dark, the door opened, and in rushed a
crowd of children laughing and shouting. They stood round
crying, 'What a pretty tree! What a pretty tree!' while the
servants lighted the candles, one by one, and a great ring of

light glowed and shimmered about the little tree. But even as the fir tree stretched and spread and felt itself a king at last, a candle flame leapt and burned into the greenery, and there was a sharp pain. Then the children began to dance about until the tree felt faint and giddy, and at last a voice cried, 'Blow the candles out!' All the children rushed up, huffing and blowing, and next minute the tree was in darkness again.

The lamps were lit and the children began to strip the tree, tugging with eager fingers at the gifts and the golden apples and the bags of sweets until the fir tree's boughs were bruised and aching. At last it was quite bare and everyone went away and the tree was left there alone and forgotten.

'What will happen now?' it wondered. 'Perhaps they will dress me up again tomorrow? Yes, that is what they will do. They cannot have forgotten me already!'

The night seemed long, and once or twice the fir tree, hearing the wind sighing about the house, thought of the forest, and how safe it had felt there, with its roots deep in the ground and its brothers all about.

Next day the servants pulled the fir tree roughly from the barrel and dragged it behind them up the stairs. They threw it into a dusty corner of the attic and went away. It was very silent and very dark, for there were no windows.

'Now what will happen?' wondered the little fir tree.

Nothing at all happened, except that after a time there was a scuffling and a pattering and the attic mice came out to sniff at the new arrival, whiskers atwitch.

'What are you?' they asked. 'Why are you here?'

The fir tree told them the story of how it had been brought from the forest and made king for a day, and the mice sat still and listened. And after a time, the fir tree began to tell them of the old days in the forest, of the sun and the rain and the wind, the swinging of axes and the flight of birds and the glad shouts of children. The mice sat spellbound as the tree told them its story, and the little fir tree itself began to see how free and beautiful that old life had been, out there in the sunlit forest.

As days went by, even the mice stopped coming, because the fir tree had told all the stories it knew, and they were tired of its company. So the tree leaned against the wall and dreamed about the old days, and even longed for the little hare to go bounding over its head again, and to hear children saying through a mouthful of raspberries,

'What a pretty little fir tree!'

Then, one day, the attic door opened. Hands seized the little tree and dragged it out down the stairs, and next minute the tree was out again in the open air and could feel the sun warm on its branches.

'Now a new life will begin!' cried the tree to itself, and tried to raise its worn branches to meet the sun, but they were too weak, and lay limply on the ground. But the tree could see the lime in full blossom and the swallows flying overhead and knew that the summer had come.

'Now I shall live,' it cried again. But again it was picked up and dragged to a corner of the yard among the weeds and nettles. The gold star still glittered at the top, dazzling in the sunshine.

The children who had danced round the tree at Christmas were playing in the yard. One boy ran over and tore off the gold star, crying,

'Look! Look what I've found on that ugly old Christmas tree!'

His thick boots trampled the fir tree's boughs, snapping and crunching.

The fir tree looked for the last time at the sky and the sunlight and thought,

'It is all over! I shall never see the forest again. If only I had been happy there while I had the chance! But it's too late now. Too late!'

Snap! A sharp axe bit into the tree's stem. A servant was chopping up the tree for firewood. When at last it was nothing more than a bundle of sticks it was lifted and carried in bundles into the kitchen to make a fire under the copper.

The little fir tree snapped and cracked as the flames devoured it, and every now and then gave a long, hissing sigh,

'Too late! Too late!'

Outside in the sunlit yard the little boy who wore the golden star that was once the fir tree's crown, stood on a log with a branch in his hand for a sceptre.

'When I grow up, I shall be king!' he shouted.

'Wait, wait . . .!' whispered the fir tree from the flames. But it was too late, and soon even the fire was out.

Rapunzel

A MAN and his wife both longed to have a child. As years went by and still there was no sign of one, they began to despair. But one day the wife was down by the stream washing clothes when a frog put his head out of the water and told her that soon her wish was to be granted.

The wife was overjoyed, and hurried home to tell her husband, who immediately set about making a wooden cradle ready for the baby.

Now next to the cottage where these two lived was a great, overgrown garden, belonging to a strange old woman whom they had heardly ever seen. People said she was a witch, and were afraid of her.

One day the wife was peering over the wall into this garden when she saw a clump of green rampion growing there. Immediately she began to long for a taste of it, though she had never been particularly fond of it before.

'Dear husband, I must eat some rampion or die!' she told him when he came home from working in the forest. 'Climb over the wall and fetch me some, I beg you.'

The husband did not like the idea at all.

'It doesn't belong to us,' he told her. 'And as for that old woman who owns the garden, for all we know she may be a witch, and if she catches me out – what then?'

'What nonsense!' cried the wife. 'Witch indeed! I must have some rampion, I tell you, or I shall die!'

And so the man, although he knew full well that the old woman *was* a witch, waited until twilight and then climbed softly over the wall and began to pull up the rampion as quickly as he could. But when he straightened up to climb

back over the wall, he found himself face to face with the old witch herself, eyes a-glitter in the gloom.

'How *dare* you climb into my garden and tear up my plants!' she cried in a terrible voice. 'I have caught you red-handed, and now it will be the worse for you!'

The poor man, shaking and trembling, explained how greatly his wife had longed for the rampion, and begged the witch to forgive him.

'Never!' she cried. 'But I will make a bargain with you. Your wife is about to have a child. I will let you go free and take with you as much rampion as you like, on condition that when the child is born *I* shall have it, to bring up as my own.'

The man agreed, for he was so terrified that he hardly knew what he was saying, and scrambled safely back over the wall with the stolen rampion and a heavy heart.

Soon afterwards, a daughter was born, and when she was only a few days old the witch came and carried the child off with her. She gave her the name Rapunzel (which is another name for rampion.

When Rapunzel was twelve years old the witch locked her in a tall stone tower that stood in the thickest and darkest part of a great wood. It had neither staircase nor doors, only a little window in Rapunzel's own room right at the very top.

Whenever the witch wanted to enter, she would stand below and call up,

'Rapunzel, Rapunzel, let down your hair!'

Rapunzel had long yellow hair, which she wore in plaits wound about her head. When she heard the witch, she would twist them round a hook by the window and let them down. They fell like thick golden ropes, and the witch would climb up by them.

When Rapunzel had been in the tower for several years it happened one day that the king's son rode by. He heard a beautiful voice singing nearby, and pushing his way through the dim green thicket came for the first time upon the lonely sunless tower. Rapunzel's voice drifted down from the little window, and she sang so sweetly of her loneliness that the Prince longed to join her. He searched about the tower to find a door, but in vain, and in the end he was forced to ride away.

After that, he would often ride in the wood and make his way to the tower in its secret

thicket. And one day, while he
was hidden there among the
laurel leaves, the old witch herself appeared, and he heard her
call out,

'Rapunzel, Rapunzel, let down
your hair!'

The Prince saw Rapunzel's
face at the high window, he saw
her lift her hands to unpin her
braids, and a minute later the
golden ropes of hair came tumbling to the ground. The witch
climbed up while the Prince
watched.

'If that is the ladder that will
take me up to that fair lady, then
I shall try my own luck,' he
thought.

Next day he went at evening
into the forest and came to the
tower in the half darkness. He
called from the shadow of the
thicket in a voice as hoarse as the
witch's own,

'Rapunzel, Rapunzel, let down
your hair!'

Then at last he was grasping
the smooth warm ropes of hair
and climbing upwards and into
the little stone room.

Rapunzel was terrified when
first she saw him, for she had
never so much as set eyes on a
man before. But the Prince

spoke gently to her, telling how he had come each day to
hear her sing, and how his heart had been won by her song.
When he told her that he wished to take her away and marry
her, he looked so kind and handsome that she could not help
thinking,

'He is better by far than old Mother Gothel, and surely he
will love me better.'

So she put her hand in his, and said 'Yes'.

'But I cannot escape without a ladder,' she said. 'So each
time you come, you must bring with you a skein of silk.
Then I will weave it into a ladder, and when it is long enough,
then I shall climb down by it, and you can take me away on
your horse.'

'I will come every day,' the Prince promised.

'But you must be sure to come in the evening,' Rapunzel
told him. 'Old Mother Gothel comes in the daytime, and so
she will never discover you.'

And so the Prince began to visit Rapunzel every evening,
and they would sit together in the twilight while Rapunzel
sang and wove her silken ladder. And all would have been
well for them if one day Rapunzel had not said to the witch,
quite without thinking,

'How is it, Mother Gothel, that you are twice as heavy to
draw up as the young Prince who comes at evening?'

No sooner were the words out than Rapunzel saw her

mistake, and clapped her hand to her mouth with a little cry.
But it was too late.

'What is that you say?' cried the witch in a fury. 'Wicked
girl, – have you deceived me?'

And she seized Rapunzel's beautiful hair in one hand and
with the other snatched up a pair of shears and cut off the long
plaits in two fierce snips. They fell to the floor in shining coils.

Rapunzel's tears and pleas were all in vain. The merciless
witch spirited her from the stone tower to a far-off wilderness,
where she left her to wander all alone and fend for herself.

Then, at evening, the old witch fastened the plaits of hair
to the hook by the window, and waited. Sure enough, as the
light faded, the Prince came riding into the thicket and she
heard him call,

'Rapunzel, Rapunzel, let down your hair!'

With an evil smile she let the long ropes fall.

The Prince climbed eagerly upward and in his joy he did
not notice that the golden ropes were cold as ice between his
hands. He swung over the stone sill into the little room and
was face to face with the towering witch.

'So you've come to visit your lady love!' she shrieked.
'But the pretty bird has flown, my dear, the cat has got her,
and she'll sing no more, I promise you! And as for you, the
cat shall scratch out *your* eyes, too! Rapunzel is gone forever,
and you shall never set eyes on her again!'

At this the Prince was so beside himself with grief and despair that he threw himself down from the window. He fell into the dark thicket, and though he was not killed, the sharp thorns scratched out his eyes and he was left in darkness.

Alone and blind he wandered the woods, living on roots and berries and lamenting the loss of his bride. Years and years went by, until at last he came to that very wilderness

where Rapunzel had been cast by the witch and where she was still living.

As he went in darkness he heard a sweet voice singing and knew instantly that he had found Rapunzel, and called her name out loud.

She came running to him and fell into his arms, weeping. Two of her warm tears fell upon his eyes and in that moment he could see as well as ever before, and the very first thing he saw with his new eyes was Rapunzel's face.

Then he took her away to his own kingdom where they were welcomed with great rejoicing and married at last, to live long and happily together.

Hansel and Grettel

THERE was once a poor woodcutter who lived with his second wife and his two children at the edge of a great forest. He was so very poor that often there was no dinner or supper either, and at last the day came when there was no food left in the pantry but a single loaf.

That night the wife said, 'It is no use, husband. You cannot make a living for four of us with your axe. If there were only two of us, then we might manage.'

'Aye,' agreed her husband. 'What is to become of us?'

'I'll tell you,' said the woman. 'Tomorrow we must take the children deep into the forest and leave them there. We can make a fire and leave them by it with a crust of bread, and then make our way home without them.'

'Never!' cried the man. 'We cannot do such a thing!'

On and on through the night she nagged and worried until at last the man agreed to her plan.

Hansel and Grettel were lying awake in the next room because they could not sleep for hunger. When Grettel heard what their father and stepmother were plotting she began to cry bitterly, muffling her sobs under the blanket.

'Don't cry, Grettel,' said Hansel stoutly. 'I will take care of
you. We shall come safely home again, I promise you.'

He waited until the others were sleeping and then softly
rose and unlatched the door and went out. The moon was full
and it lit the pebbles at his feet so that they shone white like
daisies on the turf. Hansel stooped and gathered them in
handfuls and filled his pockets with them.

Next day at dawn the whole family set off into the forest,
but Hansel lagged behind and his father called over his shoulder,

'Hurry, Hansel, why are you dawdling?'

'I'm saying goodbye to my white cat who sits on the roof,'
replied Hansel.

'That's no cat!' his stepmother told him. 'It's the sun shining
on the wet roof!'

Hans kept behind, nonetheless, because what he was really
doing was dropping a pebble now and then along their way.
His pockets were nearly empty when at last their father said,

'We will stop here and make a fire.'

Then the stepmother gave the children a crust of bread each
and said,

'Wait here by the fire. Your father and I are going to work
nearby.'

143

Hansel and Grettel said nothing, but sat by the fire and looked at one another. They waited for a long time, and every now and then they thought they heard the sound of an axe swinging. But it was really a loose branch that was blowing in the wind against the bark of another tree.

It began to grow dark and Hansel and Grettel ate their crusts of bread and gathered more sticks. Soon there was only one little ring of light left in the whole forest, about their own fire. The wild beasts howled in the darkness beyond. Grettel began to cry.

'Don't cry,' said Hansel, putting his arm about her shoulders. 'Soon the moon will be up, and then you'll see!'

Slowly the moon rose above the forest trees and Hansel stood up and pointed down to the pebbles he had thrown from his pocket.

'See how they shine!' cried Grettel.

All the way home the stones shone in a silver trail before them, bright as new shillings.

'Where have you been, you bad children?' cried their stepmother when they arrived home at dawn. She behaved just as if it were all *their* fault. But Hansel and Grettel wisely said nothing at all, and could tell that their father was pleased to see them again.

Things went on much as before for several months, when again the family fell on hard times and only a single stale loaf stood in the larder. That night, Hansel and Grettel, lying awake in the dark, heard their stepmother plotting again. At first their father would not listen, but in the end he had to give in and agree that the next day they would leave the children in the forest again. As soon as they fell asleep, Hansel got up, but this time the door was locked and so he had to go back to bed and think of another plan.

'Don't worry,' he told his sister. 'I shall think of something.'

Next day, before they left for the forest, their stepmother gave them each a crust of bread. And again, as they went on their way, Hansel lagged behind and his father called out.

'Why are you dawdling? Hurry up!'

Hansel replied, 'I'm only looking at the white dove that is sitting on the roof to say goodbye!'

'That's no dove!' cried the stepmother. 'It's the sun, shining on the wet roof!'

But what Hansel was really doing, was breaking his crust into crumbs and dropping them now and then to mark their way, as he had done with the pebbles.

This time Hansel and Grettel were not so frightened, because they had found their own way back once, and thought that they could do it again. They sat by the fire and waited

till the moon came up, and then Hansel went in search of his trail of crumbs. But the thousand hungry birds of the forest had come down and eaten them up, every single one. The path towards home had gone.

Grettel began to cry again, but Hansel tried to appear braver than he felt and said,

'Lie by the fire and go to sleep. Soon it will be morning and we shall easily find our way home.'

They lay down and fell asleep. When morning came they set off and Hansel was sure they were going the right way because he remembered a clump of silver birches they had passed the day before. But in a forest there are many clumps of silver birches, and in reality Hansel and Grettel were going deeper and deeper into the forest and soon were more lost than ever. As they travelled along they searched for wild berries to eat, and they sang songs to keep up their spirits. But by nightfall they were right in the middle of the wood and were forced to stop and light a fire to keep off the wild beasts.

Next day the two children set bravely off again, but by now they were so tired and hungry that they could hardly walk.

'It's no use, brother!' cried Grettel at last. 'I can go no further!'

Hansel did not hear her. He was pointing ahead to something he could glimpse through the trees, and pulling at his sister's hand he began to hurry towards it. They both stopped and stood staring.

It was a little house with walls of gingerbread and a roof of cake and windows of frosted sugar. Hansel ran forward and broke off a piece of the roof in a shower of crumbs,

'Food!' he cried, his cheeks bulging, and Grettel too began to

stuff her mouth with the rich, curranty cake. They were snapping candy from the doorposts and licking the sticky sugar from the windows when a voice came from inside the cottage,

'Tip, tap, who goes there?'

The children answered,

'Only the wind that blows through the air!'

And they carried on eating, because they had been hungry for a long time, and felt as if they could devour the whole house between them. But a little old woman came hobbling out and cried,

'Ah! What dear, pretty little children! Are you hungry, my dears? Come along with me, and I'll find you something good!'

This old woman had built her house of gingerbread and candy on purpose to catch the eye of children wandering in the wood. But Hansel and Grettel did not know this, and they followed her gratefully indoors, stepping over a flat black cat who hissed and rose into a thin arch.

The witch (for witch she was) set out a meal of milk and pancakes and sugar and apples and nuts. Then she showed the children two little white beds into which they crept, hardly believing their luck.

In the morning the witch came and looked at them while they still slept, and smacked her lips over their rosy cheeks, muttering,

'They're a pair of dainty little morsels! Now, which is the bigger, for that one I'll eat first!'

She snatched Hansel with her bony hand and dragged him into a little pen that stood in a corner of the kitchen. There she shut him up behind the grating, cackling with glee at the thought of the fine meal she would soon have. Then she went to Grettel and gave her a shake and cried,

'Get up, lazy bones, and fetch some water and cook something nice for your brother. I want him fat, fat as can be, and the sooner he's fat, the sooner I can eat him for my dinner!'

Grettel began to cry when she saw Hansel in his cage, but she was forced to obey the wicked witch and cook him a thick rich stew full of potatoes and noodles.

'Fatter and fatter,' nodded the old witch, peering at him as he ate.

Every day Hansel was given three big meals, while Grettel herself had next to nothing, and soon was skinny as the witch's cat. But Hansel grew fatter and fatter. The witch herself could not see very well, because all witches have red eyes that are very short sighted. So each day she went to the cage and commanded,

'Hansel, put out your finger for me to feel how fat you are!'

But Hansel, instead of putting out his finger, would push an old knucklebone between the bars of the cage.

'A pity, a pity, not fat enough yet!' the old woman would grumble, and give the cat a kick.

At last, one day, the witch felt the knuckle bone for the fiftieth time and suddenly cried,

'Today! I'll have him today, fat or lean! Light the fire, girl, and put water in the pan! I'll have Hansel for my dinner, with plenty of gravy to dip the bread in!'

Poor Grettel got down on her knees and lit the fire. Hansel sat shaking with fear inside his little cage.

'We'll bake first,' said the old witch. 'I'll knead the dough, while you creep into the oven and see if it's hot enough.'

She gave Grettel a push, and stood by, so that when the girl had crept into the oven she could slam the door and cook her too, along with the bread.

'I don't see how to get in,' said Grettel, who knew very well what would happen to her if she did climb in.

'Goose!' shrieked the witch. 'Simpleton! Anyone could do it! Look – like this!'

She hobbled to the oven and put her head and shoulders right inside and Grettel came up behind her and gave a great push and bang went the oven door! The witch was inside! She let out such a howl that the ribby cat gave one last sizzling hiss and shot out of the cottage and away into the forest, his tail stiff as a poker with fright. Hansel stamped his feet with delight and rattled at the bars of his cage.

'Hurrah!' he cried. 'Bravo! The old witch is dead and roasted! Serve her right! And good riddance to the old cat, too! Let me out now, let me out!'

Grettel ran and undid the latch and they both danced round laughing and crying, one fat and the other thin but both merry as larks to be free again at last.

In the cottage they found chests full of treasure, and Hansel stuffed his pockets with pearls and precious stones. Grettel filled her apron with gold and silver pieces and then broke off a big hunk of cake from the cottage roof to last them till they were home.

Off they set, and as if by magic this time they found the right way, and by nightfall could see their father's house in the distance with a candle burning in the window.

Their father was overjoyed to see them alive and well, and told them that their stepmother was now dead.

'But if you will forgive me, the three of us can live together again, and whatever we have in the world, even if it is but a crust, we will share it.'

'Then we'll start by sharing this!' cried Grettel, and she let her apron drop and all the gold and silver went raining down to the earthen floor under her father's astonished eyes. Hansel turned his pockets inside out and rubies and pearls flew to all four corners of the hut.

'Praise be!' cried the good woodman. 'Now we can be happy!'

And so they were, ever after.

Beauty and the Beast

THERE was once a wealthy merchant who had lost his wife but had three sons and three daughters. The sons were fine young men and the three girls were all beautiful, but the youngest in particular was so lovely that right from being a little child she had been called 'Beauty'. She was as kind and wise as she was beautiful, and her elder sisters, who were vain and proud, were both jealous of her.

Then the merchant lost his fortune and all he had left was a cottage in the country with a few acres of land around it. He called his children together and told them what had happened.

'We must go and live in the cottage,' he told them, 'and make our living as honestly as we may, and try to be happy.'

The two elder daughters laughed the idea to scorn.

'Live in the *country*?' cried they. 'In a *cottage*? That is hardly the life for us! We shall get married.'

But now that they had no fortune, nobody wanted to marry them, and so they were forced to go to the country after all. The family settled in the cottage and the merchant and his sons set to work to dig and till the land. Beauty herself rose at four every morning and spent the whole day cleaning and cooking and looking after her hens. The only ones who were bored were the two sisters, who got up late and then spent the whole day idling and talking about the old days when they had been rich and gone to fine balls every night of the week.

After a year or so the merchant had a letter to tell him that a ship on which he had valuable cargo had come safely into port. Overjoyed, he prepared himself for the journey to go and collect the money. Before he left, he called his three daughters and asked each of them what she would like him

to bring back as a present. The two elder sisters greedily prepared such long lists of gowns and hats and mantles that their poor father secretly wondered if there would be any money left once he had bought them all.

When it came to Beauty's turn to choose, she did not wish to ask for anything at all, but knew her sisters would think her priggish if she asked for nothing, so she replied,

'I wish I could have a rose – just a single rose. There are none in our garden here in the country, and I long to see and smell one again.'

The father set off with high hopes, but when he reached the port he found that he still owed so much money that when he had paid it all, there was nothing left. So he turned back home no richer than he had started, and was sad at heart to think that he could not afford to buy the presents he had promised his children.

When he was only thirty miles from home, and riding through a great forest, it began to snow. The flakes whirled so thickly that he could see only a few yards before him, and soon he had taken a wrong turning and was quite lost. It was

growing dark, and far off he heard the wolves howl. He stumbled, and fell into the snow, and lay there for a minute in despair. Then he began to pull himself to his feet, and lifted his head and saw golden bands of light shining through the curtain of snow. He made towards them and soon he saw that the light shone from hundreds of windows of a great castle, and thankfully he led the horse within the stone walls of the courtyard. There the door of a stable stood open, and he saw a manger filled with corn and hay. The tired horse trotted gratefully inside and was soon well fed and ready for the night.

The merchant himself then went to the house, but there was not a sign of life. All was brilliantly lit and warm, but absolutely silent. He pushed the door and went in and found himself in a dining hall where a fire blazed and a table stood set ready for one person. He went to the fire and warmed himself and cast longing looks towards the fine supper, but though he waited and waited, nobody came. By eleven o'clock he was so ravenously hungry that he said to himself,

'Surely, whoever is master here will pardon me if I take some food?'

And he went and took some chicken and then some wine and some fruit and soon began to feel better. He went out and began to explore the palace and soon found himself in a rich apartment set out ready as if for a guest. Here he lay on the bed and was soon asleep.

When he awoke next morning the first thing he saw was a new suit of clothes laid where his own wet and muddy things had been the night before.

'This palace must surely belong to a good fairy,' thought he. He dressed and went down to find a fire blazing and the table set with hot toast and steaming chocolate.

When he had eaten the merchant went out to his horse and saw that the snow had all gone and the sun was shining over green lawns and curving fountains and great banks of beautiful roses. At the sight of the flowers he suddenly remembered Beauty's parting wish, and as he went under an archway, reached up and snapped off a single red rose.

As he did so there came a terrible roar and the merchant turned to find himself face to face with a beast so horrible that he almost fainted right away with terror.

'So this is your gratitude!' snarled the Beast. 'I have saved your life by taking you in to my castle, and you repay me by robbing me of my roses, that I love more than anything else in the world! And you shall die for it!'

The merchant threw himself on his knees.

'Pardon me, my lord! I meant no harm! I was only plucking a single rose to take to one of my daughters who had asked me to bring her one!'

'I am not called "My Lord," but "The Beast,"' snarled the terrible creature then. 'And whether you meant to take one rose or a thousand makes not a whit of difference. But you say you have daughters at home. Very well. If one of them will come willingly here, and give her life in your place, then you may go free. But if none of them will do this, you must give me your promise that you will return here yourself three months from this day.'

The merchant had no intention of letting one of his daughters die instead of himself, but he thought, 'This gives me at least a chance to go and see them for the last time, and say my farewells,' and so he agreed, and gave his promise. Then the Beast told him to go back to his room in the castle, where he would find an empty chest.

'Fill it with as much treasure as you can carry,' said the Beast. 'There is no need for you to go away empty handed.'

With this he disappeared. And so the merchant rode home laden with riches after all, though his heart was sadly laden too.

When he reached home his family rushed to welcome him and the two elder sisters clamoured for their gifts. The merchant shook his head and took the rose and gave it to Beauty, saying,

'Take your rose, my Beauty, and enjoy it while you may, for it has cost your poor father very dear!'

Then he told them the whole story, and when he had finished the two elder sisters cried,

'There! See now what you have done, Beauty, with your childish requests!'

The three brothers cried,

'Only tell us where this monster lives, and we will go and kill him!'

'He would kill *you*,' replied the merchant. 'No, there is nothing else for it. I must die.'

But when the three months were up, Beauty went with her father to the Beast's castle determined that she would take his place. No one could stop her, and as the pair left the cottage the brothers wept and the two sisters cried tears they had made by rubbing their eyes with an onion.

The merchant's horse guided the pair to the Beast's palace of his own accord, and they found it brightly lit as before. A fine meal was set out for two people and they sat to their supper, though they were too sad to be hungry and only ate each to please the other. As they rose from the table there was a terrible growling, and there stood the Beast himself before them. He asked Beauty whether she had come readily, of her own free will, to take her father's place, and when she answered 'Yes', he said to her,

'You are a good girl, and I am obliged to you.'

Then he told the merchant that he might stay in the palace

for the night, but that next morning he was to go and never return again.

When Beauty had parted from her father next morning, she threw herself down and wept bitterly. When she was calmer she sat up and looked about her and began to wonder what strange kind of place this was. She walked through the lovely gardens and then explored the palace itself. The more she saw, the more she had the strange feeling that it had all been planned specially for herself, and no one else. Even her favourite books stood upon the shelves and the rooms were furnished with the colours she loved best. She took down one of the books, and read in gold letters,

'Desire. Command. You are Lady and Mistress here.'

'Alas!' sighed Beauty. 'All I desire is to see my poor father and know how he is.'

She laid down the book and looked up, straight into a large mirror that hung on the wall opposite. There, in the glass, she saw the cottage and her father entering it, his face full of grief. Then her sisters ran out to greet him, and as she watched the picture faded and they were gone. But now her heart was lighter, for she thought,

'The Beast is perhaps not so fierce as he seems. Surely if he were, he would not have done such a thing to make me happy?'

At supper that evening the Beast appeared again and though Beauty trembled with terror she forced herself to look at him and answer his questions.

'Beauty,' growled the monster, 'are you willing to let me look at you while you sup?'

'You are master here,' replied Beauty.

'No!' replied the Beast. 'You alone are mistress here. If you bid me go away, I shall go. And it would be no great surprise if you did so. Tell me, am I not the ugliest thing you ever set eyes on?'

'You *are* ugly,' agreed Beauty, not wishing to tell a lie. 'But I begin to think that you are very kind. And when I think how good you are at heart, then you no longer seem quite so ugly to me.'

The Beast seemed pleased by her words and sat quite still and watched while she finished her supper. Then, quite without warning, he said,

'Beauty, will you be my wife?'

She was so shocked by the question that at first she could find no words to answer, but replied simply at last,

'No, Beast.'

At this he let out a shriek of pain so terrible that the whole palace shook and Beauty thought her last hour had come. But the Beast, once he had recovered, only said gently,

'Goodnight, then, Beauty,' and went to the door, with a last wistful look at her before he went. Beauty, seeing his large, reproachful eyes, was filled with pity.

'Poor Beast,' she thought. 'To be so kind of heart and yet to be so ugly.'

Three months passed by, and each day Beauty amused herself in the palace and gardens, and each evening the Beast came to visit her. As the days passed, she became used to his ugliness and even began to look forward to seeing him at night. There was only one thing she dreaded, and that was the time when, before he left her, he would ask her the same question, night after night.

'Beauty, will you marry me?'

And each night she was forced to answer 'No,' and

to see his pain and sadness. One evening she said to him,

'Beast, I only wish that I *could* marry you, but I cannot bring myself to pretend what I do not feel. I shall always be your friend – can you not be content with that?'

'I suppose I must,' replied the Beast. 'And I cannot blame you, for I know how horribly ugly I am. But I love you more than life itself – will you at least promise me that you will never leave me?'

Now that very day Beauty had looked into the magic looking glass and seen there pictures of her father who had become ill with grief at losing her.

'I would willingly promise never to leave you altogether!' she cried. 'But I long so much to see my poor father again that I fear both he and I will die of grief if I cannot visit him!'

'I would rather die myself than make you unhappy,' said the Beast. 'But if I send you home, then you will never come back, and then your poor Beast will die of grief!'

'Oh no!' cried Beauty, weeping. 'I love you too much now to wish to cause your death. If you let me go to my father, I promise I shall return in eight days.'

'You shall be there in the morning,' the Beast told her. 'And when you wish to return, lay your ring on the table before you go to bed. And remember your promise, Beauty – eight days. Goodbye!'

The Beast gave his usual great sigh and left her for the night, and when he had gone Beauty went to bed and wept into her pillow, grieved that she should have hurt him. When she awoke next day she was in her father's house, and the whole household was amazed at her marvellous reappearance. Her father was beside himself with joy, and begged Beauty to hurry and dress and come downstairs so that they would have the whole long day together.

Then Beauty realised that she had no clothes to put on, but the maid came and told her that she had just found a chest in the next room, and that it was filled with beautiful

and costly gowns. Beauty's eyes filled with tears as she
remembered the poor, ugly Beast and saw how well and
faithfully he looked after her.

Beauty's father was soon well again, and one day her sisters
came visiting with their husbands. They were filled with spite
and envy when they saw Beauty looking so happy, lovelier
than ever and dressed like a princess. When they learned of
the promise Beauty had made to the Beast, they began to
plot against her.

'We will persuade her to overstay her visit,' said the eldest.
'Then the Beast will be so enraged that he will devour her,
and we shall be rid of her forever!'

'Perfect!' cried the other. 'We will pretend to be very fond
of her, and beg her to stay longer with us, and she is so soft-
hearted that she is bound to give in!'

And so it happened. On the eighth day, when Beauty was
preparing to leave, her sisters made such a show of grief and
wept so loudly and implored her so desperately to stay

longer with them, that Beauty was quite overwhelmed.

'I had not known that they loved me so dearly,' she thought. 'And surely there is no great harm in staying just a little longer, to make them happy?'

And so she gave in and stayed, and the wicked sisters gloated secretly and were certain that soon she would pay for it with her life.

But on the tenth night of her visit, Beauty had a dream. She dreamed that she saw the Beast lying weak and dying in the grass, and reproaching her for breaking her promise to him. Beauty woke with a start and began to weep.

'Poor Beast!' she cried. 'How could I be so wicked and thoughtless! Ugly as he is, he has shown me nothing but gentleness and kindness, and this is how I repay him!'

She took off her ring, placed it on the table beside the bed, and went to sleep again. When she awoke, she was back in her room at the Beast's palace.

She spent the day happily enough and towards evening went and dressed in her most beautiful gown to give the Beast pleasure, and eagerly went down to supper to meet him.

The clock struck nine, the Beast did not appear. Beauty knew at once that something was amiss, and began to run about the empty palace, vainly calling his name. Then she ran out into the gardens, remembering that in her dream she had seen the Beast lying in the grass near the brook. And it was there that she found him, lying with his eyes closed, looking as though he were already dead.

Beauty ran and flung herself to her knees beside him. She lifted his great head and cradled it in her lap, stroking it and weeping and crying,

'Oh Beast, Beast, my dear Beast, what have I done to you?'

She thought she saw his eyelids flicker, and ran straightway to the brook for water to wet her handkerchief. Then she bathed his forehead, murmuring his name as she did so, and at last the Beast's eyes opened and he looked up at her.

'You forgot your promise,' he said faintly. 'But now that I have seen you once more, I shall die happy, looking on your beloved face.'

'No, dear Beast, you shan't die,' cried Beauty. 'You must live and become my husband. I know now that I love you truly, and want nothing more than to become your wife and make you happy. You must live, Beast, for my sake!'

No sooner had she spoken these words than the whole palace was suddenly lit from within and beautiful music began to play. She turned her head to look, and when she looked back to the place where the Beast had been lying an instant before, there knelt a young Prince, bright as the day.

'Where is my Beast?' cried Beauty.

'I am he,' came the reply. 'Thanks to you, dear Beauty, I am a Beast no more. I was doomed by a wicked fairy to take the shape of a horrible beast until of her own free will someone should come to love me and consent to marry me.'

And so Beauty and her Prince went together into the lighted palace where they found her father, and were married in his presence that very day.

As for the wicked sisters, they were turned into stone statues and forced to stand forever, one each side of the palace door, and watch their sister living happily with her Prince for the rest of her days.

The Emperor's New Clothes

ONCE upon a time there lived an Emperor whose greatest delight in life was the wearing and showing off of his rich clothes. It was all he really cared about. If he went to the theatre, or for a drive through the streets, it was only because he wanted everyone to see and admire him. He changed his clothes half a dozen times a day, and often his courtiers, instead of saying 'The Emperor's in the Council' would say, 'The Emperor's in the Wardrobe.'

One day, two travellers came to the court.

'We beg to be allowed to make Your Excellency a new suit of clothes,' they said. 'We make the most beautiful clothes in the world, and the one we should like to weave for you is a very special one indeed.'

'Indeed? Tell me about it,' replied the Emperor, preening himself.

'It is beautiful beyond compare,' said the weavers. 'But that is not all. It can only be seen by those who are clever and wise and well suited to their jobs. Those who are dull or stupid or not fit to do their jobs, can't see a single thing. It's quite invisible to them.'

'Invisible?' exclaimed the Emperor.

'Invisible,' nodded the two men.

'Now this will be very interesting,' thought the Emperor. 'For one thing, I shall have another fine new suit of clothes. For another, I shall be able to find out who is clever and who is stupid.'

'It will be very expensive,' added one of the two men. 'Naturally. And we shall require a thousand gold pieces in advance.'

The Emperor gave orders that the two men were to be given a loom and all the materials they asked for. They set the loom up in a room in the palace and began to order vast quantities of silks and threads – especially *gold* threads. As soon as these arrived, they stuffed them all into their bags and began to work at the empty looms all day and well into the night.

The Emperor could hardly wait to see his new suit. But every time he thought about it he had a queer sinking feeling inside him, when he remembered that it would be quite invisible to anyone who was stupid or not fitted for his job.

'Not, of course, that it could possibly apply to me,' he thought. 'Everyone says how clever I am, and of course I am the very man to be Emperor!'

All the same, he kept away from the room where the men were working. On the second day he could contain his curiosity no longer and sent one of his most trusted ministers to see how the work was going.

'He will certainly be able to see the cloth,' the Emperor told himself. 'A wiser man I have never known.'

The old Minister went into the room were the work was

going on and stared in amazement at the sight of two men busily working away at what looked like a perfectly empty loom. He rubbed his eyes. Still the loom was empty.

'Dear me,' thought the Minister, 'Am I really so stupid? But whatever happens, I mustn't admit it. I must pretend to see the cloth and admire it, to show the world how wise I am, and how well suited to my job!'

'Well, do you like it?' asked one of the men, stepping back as if to admire his work.

'O gracious, yes!' cried the old man. 'Upon my word! I hardly know what to say! What colours, what a design, what a perfectly *ravishing* piece of work!'

'We thought you would like it,' said the cunning pair. 'Perhaps you'll be good enough to tell his Excellency how well it's going? And while you're at it, we shall need a few more thousand yards of gold thread, and a couple of sacks of pearls.'

'O certainly, yes, certainly!' agreed the Minister. 'I shall see to it at once!'

Off he went, quite bewildered, and more than a little sad, because he had always tried to serve the Emperor wisely and well, and now it seemed that he was nothing but a simpleton.

But even if he were stupid, there was no point in telling everyone so, and he assured the Emperor that the cloth being woven for his new suit was quite the most exquisite he had ever seen in his whole life.

'Good,' thought the Emperor. 'My Minister is a wise man.'

But still he was not quite ready to face seeing the cloth himself, and next day he sent two courtiers to see how the work was going. By now, everyone in the kingdom had heard of the wonderful cloth that could be seen only by the wise and the clever. The two courtiers came back rather pale, but praising the work highly, and bringing an order for still more gold thread and silks.

At last the day came when the Emperor simply had to go and see for himself. He went into the room, and there were the two men working away for dear life on a loom that had not a single thread or stitch to be seen! The Emperor was horrified.

'I'm a fool!' he thought. 'I'm a simpleton! I'm unfit for my job! O dear, O dear!'

But he forced a smile to his lips, because everyone was watching him to see what he would say.

'Ravishing!' he said at last. No one spoke. 'Ravishing!' he said again, more loudly this time, and immediately all the

courtiers and officials who were with him began saying to one another,

'Ravishing! Wonderful! Miraculous! Out of this world!'

'I shall appoint you Lord High Weavers,' said the Emperor, and gave each of the men a medal to pin on his suit.

'Your Excellency must wear a suit made of this cloth for the Grand Procession next week!' said the Chief Courtier, determined not to be outdone in praising the cloth. After all, he told himself, if the *Emperor* could see the cloth, it *must* be there!

'O — should I?' said the Emperor. 'You don't think my scarlet silk, with the gold lace cuffs and — '

'No, Your Excellency, with respect,' said the Chief Courtier. 'This very cloth. You owe it to your people. They have all heard of this wonderful cloth, and can hardly wait to see it. At least,' he coughed behind his hand, 'the *wise* ones can hardly wait to see it!'

The court laughed merrily and the Emperor himself managed to force out a titter.

Before the Grand Procession the two weavers worked all night with sixteen candles burning. They pretended to take the cloth from the loom, their great scissors clipped at the air, and they stitched busily with empty needles. No one could doubt that they were actually making a suit of clothes.

Then the Emperor arrived with his courtiers. The weavers bowed before him with a great flourish and then held out their arms saying, 'Here is the coat, here are the breeches, and this is the cloak! We beg you to try them, for we're sure you'll be delighted. You won't even know you have anything on, because the cloth is so fine that it's light as gossamer!'

The Emperor took off the clothes he was wearing and they pretended to put on him the clothes they had made.

'How does that feel?' they asked, and 'It's not too tight is it, Your Excellency?'

'O no, no, I assure you!' cried the Emperor, craning and peering before the glass in the hope that he might catch a

glimpse of the suit and prove himself not such a fool after all. 'It's the most comfortable suit I have ever worn.'

'The fit is wonderful!' sighed the courtiers, shaking their heads. 'And as for the colours! And the design! Magnificent!'

Two chamberlains stooped and picked up the invisible train. The Emperor was ready.

Outside the palace the streets were packed with excited people all waiting for the first glimpse of the Emperor's new clothes.

The Emperor stepped out of the palace and felt his skin break out into a rash of goose pimples. There was a short silence, and then a great cheer went up. People leaned out of windows, crying,

'Hurrah! Hurrah for the Emperor's new clothes!'

'Just look at that coat!'

'What style, what colours, what fit!'

Not a single person there was ready to admit that in fact he could see nothing at all. Every man shouted more loudly than his neighbour, to prove that he could see the clothes and was clever and wise and fitted for his job.

The Emperor himself, deafened by the applause and shouting, was just beginning to rid himself of a strong suspicion that he was walking out stark naked, when a child's voice rang out from the crowd,

'But he's got nothing on!'

There was a hush. The Emperor kept his eyes fixed ahead and felt the goose pimples break out afresh. The voice came again in the silence, clear and high, because it came from a little child who didn't care a fig whether he was thought wise or not.

'He hasn't got anything *on*!'

A whispering went through the crowd.

'There's a child here says the Emperor's got nothing on! Not a stitch on, he says!'

The whisper grew louder, it hissed like waves on the shingle,

'Not a stitch on! Nothing on at all!'

Until at last they all shouted out together,

'Why, but he hasn't anything on at all!'

The Emperor groaned inwardly, for he knew they were right. He only needed his goose pimples to tell him that. But he was, after all, the Emperor, so he pretended not to have heard. He drew himself up more proudly than ever and walked on, with the chamberlains stiffly behind him, bearing the train that wasn't even there.

Tom Thumb

THERE were once two good people who longed to have a child of their own.

'I wouldn't care even if he were no bigger than my thumb,' said the wife one evening as she turned her spinning wheel.

And that was exactly how it turned out, because not very long afterwards the wife *did* have a son, and although he grew strong and healthy, he was no bigger than her thumb. They were both delighted with their tiny son, and gave him the name of Tom Thumb.

As he grew up, Tom himself sometimes used to wish that he were bigger, so that he could be more help to his mother and father.

One day, his father was going off to chop wood in the forest, and he said to his wife,

'I wish there were someone who could bring the cart to me in the forest, to carry the wood.'

'I'll bring it, father!' cried Tom, who had overheard him.

'You will?' said his father. 'You aren't even big enough to hold on to the reins!'

'I know that,' replied Tom Thumb. 'But let me try.'

'Very well,' his father agreed. 'We shall see.'

In the afternoon, Tom asked his mother to harness the horse to the cart, and to lift him up into the horse's ear. There he perched, clutching tightly on to the warm leather and seeing the horse's nose far away below.

Tom Thumb took a deep breath.

'Gee-up!' he cried, and off went the horse at a trot. All the way to the wood Tom guided the horse by shouting into his ear, and began to think himself no end of a fine fellow. As

173

they drew near the wood, two strange men were standing by the roadside.

'That's queer!' said one to the other. 'There goes a horse and cart, and there's someone calling to the horse, and yet there's not a sign of a driver!'

'We'll follow,' said the other. 'And see what happens.'

When Tom reached the clearing where his father was at work he called out to him,

'Here I am, father! I've done it, you see!'

His father looked round in astonishment, and proudly lifted Tom down from the horse's ear. At this, the two men who had been following could hardly believe their eyes.

'Would you believe it?' cried the first. 'A little man no bigger than your thumb! What a fortune we could make if we could only take him to the town and show him off in a fair or circus!'

'We must try to buy him,' agreed the second. 'If we do, our fortunes are surely made.'

But when they spoke to Tom's father and offered him gold if he would part with his son, the good man would not even hear of it.

'He's our only son!' he cried. 'We wouldn't part with him for all the gold in the world!'

He lifted Tom on to his shoulder as he spoke, but Tom
whispered in his ear,

'Take the gold, father. Pretend to sell me. I'll be home
again by nightfall, never fear!'

So in the end the two men gave Tom's father a fine large
piece of gold, and he handed over his son in exchange. One
of the men put Tom in the brim of his hat and they set off
with Tom waving cheerfully to his father. Towards nightfall,

the men began looking for somewhere to sleep, and saw the
lights of a village ahead.

'You must lift me down!' cried Tom then. 'I'm dizzy!'

So they took him out of the hat brim and set him on the
ploughed furrows of the field they were crossing, and before
they had even time to blink Tom had darted off and scurried
down a mousehole.

'Goodbye, gentlemen!' he called. 'You'll have to make
your own fortunes, I fear!'

The two men got down on hands and knees and peered
about in the twilight, poking and prodding with sticks and
muttering angrily under their breath. But Tom Thumb lay
snug and safe in his straw-lined mousehole, and when at last

the men gave up and went away, he climbed gleefully out.

He began to set off towards home, but the furrows rolled like mountains on all sides, and he thought to himself,

'I must find somewhere to sleep. I daren't cross this field in the dark – I could easily break a leg – or even my neck!'

On the other side of the very next furrow he found an empty snail shell.

'The very thing!' thought Tom. He curled himself roundly into it, and was beginning to doze when he heard voices nearby.

'How can we set about stealing the rich parson's gold and silver?' said one.

Immediately Tom Thumb was wide awake again and popped his head out of the shell.

'I'll tell you!' he cried.

'What was that?' cried the second robber in alarm.

'It's me!' cried Tom. 'Here! Look down here! I'm in this snail shell. But mind you don't tread on me!'

The robbers bent and peered on the ground and at last found Tom Thumb and lifted him up.

'*You're* an odd little fellow!' cried the first robber. 'How can *you* help us?'

'I can creep between the iron bars on the windows,' said Tom. 'And then I can pass all the gold and silver out to you.'

'So you could!' cried the robbers, delighted by the plan. 'You may be small, but you're a clever little fellow, and shall have a share of the treasure yourself if you do the job well.'

Off they set to the parson's house, and when they came to it the robbers put Tom through the window between the iron bars, and waited outside, ready to put the treasure into their sacks as Tom handed it out. But once Tom was inside, he called out in a very loud voice,

'Do you want me to steal everything?'

'Ssssh!' hissed the robber. 'Not so loud! They'll hear you!'

'That's just what I want,' thought tricky Tom Thumb, and he shouted again, louder than ever,

'There's plenty of gold and silver here! Shall I steal it all?'

'Ssssh!' hissed the robbers again, looking nervously about them.

In the room upstairs, the maid woke up.

'What was that?' she wondered. 'Is there someone downstairs, stealing the master's treasure?'

Sure enough, the very next moment, there was Tom's voice again, and the maid jumped up and ran downstairs shouting 'Help! Thieves! Murder!'

The robbers waited to hear no more. They took to their heels and did not stop running till they were more than a mile away. As for Tom, he waited until the maid had gone to fetch a light, then crept out of the window and went across to the barn, where he was soon fast asleep in the deep hay.

Unluckily for Tom, he had crept into the very bundle of hay that had been put there ready to feed the cow. He was so soundly asleep that he did not hear the maid come down and carry the hay over to the cow's stall. When he woke up, he was right inside the cow's jaws.

'Help!' he cried. 'Where am I?'

The cow swallowed, and Tom went right down with the hay. It was very hot and dark and uncomfortable down in the cow's stomach, and to make matters worse, more and more hay kept coming down until Tom could hardly find room to breathe. So he began to cry out,

'Don't give me any more hay! Don't give me any more hay!'

The poor maid thought the voice she heard belonged to the cow, and was scared out of her wits. She ran to the parson, shrieking,

'Master, master, come quick! The cow's bewitched!'

The parson himself came running, and the first thing he heard was Tom's muffled voice,

'Don't give me any more hay!'

'The cow *is* bewitched!' the parson cried. 'It must be killed at once!'

So the cow was killed and the stomach thrown on to a rubbish heap in the yard. Tom set about finding his way out, and had just managed to poke out his head and was gulping in the sweet fresh air, when along came a wolf. He opened his great jaws and swallowed the cow's stomach, Tom and all, in a single, ravenous gulp!

'Out of the fry pan into the fire!' shrieked Tom Thumb, going down the wolf's long red throat in a rush. The wolf, hearing a strange voice coming from his own jaws howled in alarm and nearly deafened Tom Thumb, who stuck his fingers in his ears and waited for the noise to die down.

'Don't be afraid, wolf!' he called at last. 'It's only me, Tom Thumb! You've just swallowed me by mistake. Are you still hungry?'

'I am always hungry,' replied the wolf.

'I know of a house where you can find all the food you want,' said Tom Thumb, tricky as ever, even inside a wolf's stomach. 'There's bacon, sausages, cakes – oh, everything you could wish for!'

'You tell me,' said the greedy wolf, 'or I'll gobble you up!' – quite forgetting that he already had.

So Tom began to describe to the wolf how to reach a

certain house – and that, as you may have guessed, was his own father's house.'

'You will have to wait until night,' Tom told him, 'and then squeeze in between the gratings on the pantry window.'

So the wolf lay low until nightfall, and then did as Tom said, and was soon gobbling all the food in sight – sausages, bacon, pastry, pies. The more food went down, the better pleased Tom was.

'You had better be making off now,' he called at last, when he was sure his plan had succeeded. 'Soon it will be light, and the woodman will be coming down.'

The wolf climbed up to the window, and began to push between the iron bars. His head went through, his neck went through, but as soon as he tried to get the rest of him through, he stuck tight. The wolf had eaten so much that he was nearly twice his usual size. He puffed and panted and struggled and was still there when dawn came and the woodman and his wife came down.

When they saw the wolf in the pantry Tom's father cried,

'Quick, wife, fetch me an axe and a scythe. I will hit him on the head with the axe, and if that doesn't kill him, you must finish him off with the scythe!'

Then Tom, hearing his father's voice cried out,

'Father! Father! It's me, Tom! I'm here in the wolf's stomach! Be careful, father, or you'll kill me, too!'

'It's Tom!' cried the father, astounded. 'Put down the scythe, wife, and I'll finish him with the axe!'

He lifted the axe and brought it down on the wolf's head with a mighty blow, killing him with a single stroke. Then he eagerly set about freeing his son, and at last lifted him out and put him on the palm of his hand.

'Heaven be praised!' cried his father and mother together. 'We had given you up for lost! Where have you been all this time?'

'Down a mousehole,' replied Tom Thumb. 'In a snail shell, on a robber's shoulder, inside a cow, inside a wolf – everywhere in the wide world, I've been!'

'And now you must stay at home with us,' said his father proudly. 'We shan't sell you again, not for all the gold in the world.'

'I shall need a new suit,' said Tom Thumb. 'My old one is quite spoilt – and no wonder!'

'You have earned one,' they said. And they made him a new suit of bright yellow with a tall green hat and plume, so that Tom Thumb was the smartest – as well as the bravest – little fellow in the whole world.

The Twelve Dancing Princesses

LONG ago there was a king who had twelve beautiful daughters.
They slept in two great beds in one room, and each night the
door of this room was shut and locked. But every morning
when the princesses were woken, their shoes were found to
be quite worn out. It was as if the princesses had been out
walking – or dancing? – all night long, and yet how could
this possibly be? Nobody could think of an answer to the
mystery, and as for the princesses themselves, they simply
smiled and said not a single word.

Then the king proclaimed throughout the land that if
anyone could discover the secret, then he could choose which-
ever of the princesses he liked best to become his wife, and he
should become king himself when the old king died. But if
anyone should try for three days and three nights and still
did not succeed, then he should be put to death.

Before long a handsome prince arrived at the court to try
his luck. He was given a room next to the princesses' own,
and when he went to bed, he left the door open, so that nothing
could take place without his knowing it. He lay down on his
bed, determined to stay awake all night and watch. But

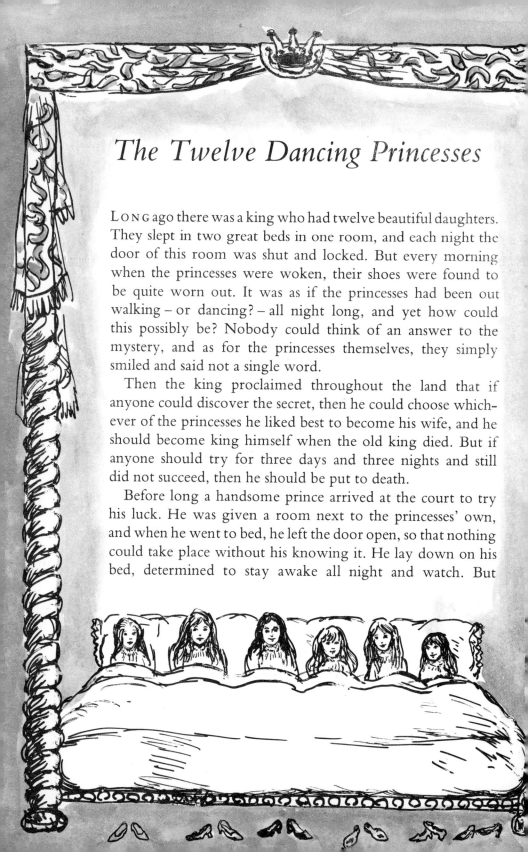

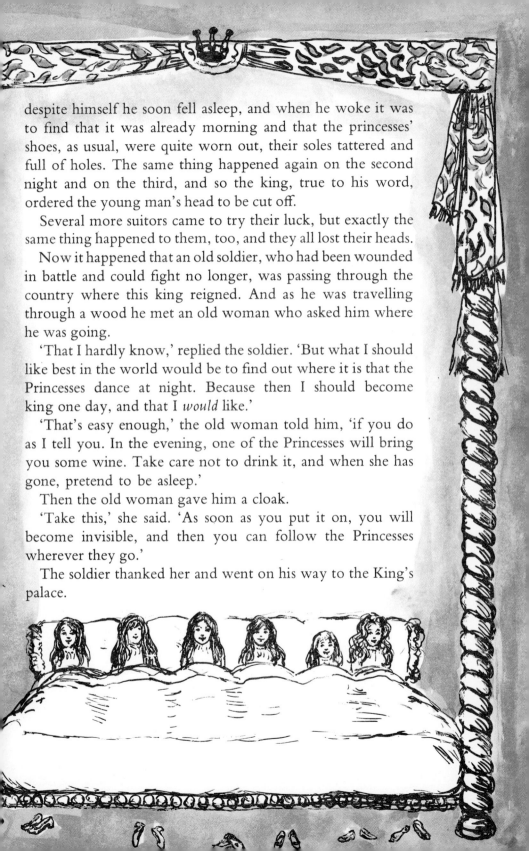

despite himself he soon fell asleep, and when he woke it was to find that it was already morning and that the princesses' shoes, as usual, were quite worn out, their soles tattered and full of holes. The same thing happened again on the second night and on the third, and so the king, true to his word, ordered the young man's head to be cut off.

Several more suitors came to try their luck, but exactly the same thing happened to them, too, and they all lost their heads.

Now it happened that an old soldier, who had been wounded in battle and could fight no longer, was passing through the country where this king reigned. And as he was travelling through a wood he met an old woman who asked him where he was going.

'That I hardly know,' replied the soldier. 'But what I should like best in the world would be to find out where it is that the Princesses dance at night. Because then I should become king one day, and that I *would* like.'

'That's easy enough,' the old woman told him, 'if you do as I tell you. In the evening, one of the Princesses will bring you some wine. Take care not to drink it, and when she has gone, pretend to be asleep.'

Then the old woman gave him a cloak.

'Take this,' she said. 'As soon as you put it on, you will become invisible, and then you can follow the Princesses wherever they go.'

The soldier thanked her and went on his way to the King's palace.

That night he was given a room next to the Princesses' own chamber. Just as he was going to lie down the eldest Princess came to him with a goblet of wine. But the soldier, remembering the words of the old woman, did not drink it, and when the Princess had gone he lay down and began to snore loudly, pretending to be asleep.

When the twelve Princesses heard this they laughed, and immediately they got up and began to dress in all their finery. They skipped and laughed and fidgeted as if they could hardly wait to begin dancing. But the youngest Princess was very quiet, and when the others asked her why, she replied,

'I do not know. But I have the strangest feeling that all is not well.'

The other Princesses only laughed and called her a simpleton.

'Just listen to him snoring!' they cried. 'We have tricked a dozen princes, haven't we? So why should we not trick this old soldier?'

They took a last peep at him as he lay snoring on his bed, and then the eldest Princess went to her bed and clapped her hands. The bed sank into the floor and a trapdoor opened. Down went the twelve Princesses, one by one, with the eldest leading. The soldier leapt up, snatched up the cloak that made him invisible, and followed them.

In his haste he trod on the gown of the youngest Princess when they were half way down the steps. She started, and cried out to her sisters,

'All is not well! Some one caught hold of my cloak!'

'Silly creature,' called the eldest over her shoulder. 'It's nothing but a nail in the wall!'

Down they went, and came out at last into a beautiful grove of trees. The leaves were all of gleaming silver, and the soldier, who had never seen such a sight before, reached and broke off a branch from a nearby tree. There was a loud snapping noise, and the youngest Princess cried,

'All is not well! Did you hear that noise?'

But the eldest replied,

'It is only our princes you hear, shouting for joy because we are coming!'

They came then into a second grove where the leaves were all of gold, and then into a third, where they glittered with diamonds. And in each grove the soldier snapped a branch from a tree, and each time the youngest Princess heard, and cried out in fear. But her sisters only laughed the more.

Soon they came to a great lake. On the water lay twelve little boats with a handsome Prince in each, and how the Princesses laughed and clapped to see them.

One of the Princesses stepped into each boat, and when it was the turn of the youngest, the soldier stepped into the boat with her.

'It is hard work rowing tonight,' remarked the Prince when they were half way over the lake. 'I am quite worn out.'

From the other side of the lake came the sound of music, silvery horns and trumpets, and the soldier saw a magnificent castle with lighted windows. And as soon as they reached the shore the twelve Princesses ran inside and soon were dancing merrily, each with her own Prince.

The soldier himself danced invisibly among them, and amused himself by playing a game. Every time one of the Princesses had a goblet of wine set by her he drank it all up, so that when she put the glass to her mouth, it was empty.

The youngest Princess was very frighted by this, but each time the eldest sister silenced her.

So they danced until cockcrow, until their slippers were quite worn out, and so they *had* to stop. The twelve Princes rowed their partners back across the lake, and this time the soldier went in the boat with the eldest Princess.

When they came to the stairs the soldier ran ahead and managed to be back in bed snoring by the time the Princesses stepped back into their own room. They peeped in and saw him there and whispered to each other,

'We're quite safe. See – he's fast asleep!'

And they pulled off their tattered slippers, yawning as they did so, and were soon fast asleep themselves.

The soldier could easily have told the secret to the King the very next day, but he wished to see more of this mysterious adventure. So he went again with the Princesses the next night, and again on the third night. But on this last visit, he took away with him a golden cup from the castle, to prove where where he had been.

Next morning he was summoned to the King, and he took with him the three branches of silver, gold and diamonds, and the golden cup. The twelve Princesses stood listening at the door, whispering and nudging each other, sure that their secret was safe.

But soon they were staring at each other round-eyed as the soldier began his tale. And when the eldest, who had her eye to the keyhole, saw him take out the three branches and the golden cup and show them to the King, she knew there was no use denying what he said. So the twelve Princesses trooped into the room and confessed the whole story to their father.

'Which of the Princesses will you choose for your wife?' asked the King, when all had been told.

'I am not so young any more,' replied the soldier, 'so I think I will choose the eldest.'

And so they were married, and in time the soldier became king of the whole country, thanks to the old woman in the woods and her good advice.

The Little Match Girl

I T was the last day of the year, and bitter cold. People hurried along the streets, their breath smoking in the frosty air, making for home and a good meal and a bright fire.

In the gloom of the evening, a little match girl was wandering barefoot and bareheaded along the pavements. She had been wearing slippers when she had set out, but they were much too big, because they had belonged to her mother. Now she had lost them both while she was jumping out of the way of a carriage. She had searched for them, but one had disappeared completely and the other had been picked up by a boy, who ran off with it, thinking he could use it as a cradle when he had children of his own.

Now the little match girl's feet were blue and red with cold, and she shivered as she held out bundles of matches to the hurrying crowds. Nobody noticed her, or even tossed her a farthing.

She crept along by the lighted windows, sniffing the delicious smell of roast goose that wafted from doorways, for it was New Year's Eve, and there was a feast set out in every house. In a corner between two houses the match girl sat down to rest, drawing her icy feet beneath her for warmth. She dared not go home, for fear of a beating. Not a single bundle of matches had she sold all day, and not a penny did she have to give to her father. Even at home she would be cold, because there were holes in the roof, and the walls were stuffed with straw and rags to stop the cold winds whistling through.

'I will light a match,' she thought. 'Perhaps that will warm me.'

With her numb fingers she drew a match from the bundle

and rubbed it against the rough stone of the wall. R-r-ratch!
It spluttered into life with a bright, warm flame like that of a
candle. The match girl cupped her hands about it, feeling a
faint warmth, and gazing into its dazzling light. It seemed to

her almost like a real stove, shining and cheerful with brass feet and a brass cover. But all at once the little flame went out, the stove vanished, and she had only the burned out end of the match in her hand.

She rubbed another against the wall. As its light fell on the wall it seemed to become transparent, like a veil, and she seemed to see right through it into the room. She saw a table spread with a snowy cloth and shining silver. She saw a glorious, smoking goose, stuffed with apples and dried plums. And as she hungrily sniffed the steam, the goose hopped down from the table with a knife and fork stuck in its side ready for her, and she gave a cry of delight and – blackness! Nothing at all. The second match had gone out.

She struck a third against the cold stone wall, and this time it showed her pictures of a Christmas tree, the biggest she had ever seen, even through the windows of the rich merchants' houses. Thousands of candles burned steadily on the thick green branches, and the little match girl stretched out her hands to warm them – and the match went out. But this time, instead of darkness, she seemed to see stars, mounting higher and higher, and then one of them fell in a long line of fire.

'Now someone is dying,' thought the little match girl. Her grandmother, who was herself dead now, had told her once that whenever a star falls down to earth a soul climbs up to God.

She rubbed another match against the wall, and this time, in the glowing ring of light she saw her old grandmother, clear and mild, smiling at her.

'Grandmother!' cried the child. 'Dear grandmother! Take me with you! I know that you will vanish when the match goes out, as the fire did, and the food, and the Christmas tree!'

Even as she spoke the grandmother began to fade, and swiftly the little match girl struck another match, and another, because she longed to keep her grandmother with her. And the matches burned so fiercely that it was bright as day and the snow was lit golden and the grandmother came nearer and nearer, holding out her arms and smiling. And the child held out her own arms, too, and smiled back.

After that, no more matches were struck. The little match girl leaned against the wall with red cheeks and smiling lips, frozen to death on the last night of the Year.

Next day the people found her there, stiff and cold, with the burned out matches scattered about her in the snow.

'Poor child!' they said. 'She was trying to warm herself.'

And no one imagined what beautiful things she had seen, and how gladly she had gone with her grandmother to the New Year's Day.